MARGUERITE HENRY'S Misty Inn

4-Books-in-1!

MARGUERITE HENRY'S Misty Inn

4-Books-in-1!

Welcome Home!
Buttercup Mystery
Runaway Pony
Finding Luck

By Kristin Earhart

Illustrated by Serena Geddes

ALADDIN
New York London Toronto Sydney New Delhi

This book is a work of fiction. Any references to historical events, real people, or real places are used fictitiously. Other names, characters, places, and events are products of the author's imagination, and any resemblance to actual events or places or persons, living or dead, is entirely coincidental.

ALADDIN

An imprint of Simon & Schuster Children's Publishing Division

1230 Avenue of the Americas, New York, New York 10020

This Aladdin hardcover edition May 2016

Welcome Home! text copyright © 2015 by Kristin Earhart

Welcome Home! illustrations copyright © 2015 by Serena Geddes

Buttercup Mystery text copyright © 2015 by Kristin Earhart

Buttercup Mystery illustrations copyright © 2015 by Serena Geddes

Runaway Pony text copyright © 2015 by Kristin Earhart

Runaway Pony illustrations copyright © 2015 by Serena Geddes

Finding Luck text copyright © 2016 by Kristin Earhart

Finding Luck illustrations copyright © 2016 by Serena Geddes

Cover illustrations copyright © 2015 by Serena Geddes

Also available in individual Aladdin hardcover and paperback editions.

All rights reserved, including the right of reproduction in whole or in part in any form.

ALADDIN is a trademark of Simon & Schuster, Inc., and related logo is a registered trademark of Simon & Schuster, Inc.

For information about special discounts for bulk purchases, please contact Simon & Schuster Special Sales at 1-866-506-1949 or business@simonandschuster.com.

The Simon & Schuster Speakers Bureau can bring authors to your live event. For more information or to book an event contact the Simon & Schuster Speakers Bureau at 1-866-248-3049 or visit our website at www.simonspeakers.com.

Designed by Laura Disiena

The text of this book was set in Century Expanded.

Manufactured in the United States of America 0416 FFG

10 9 8 7 6 5 4 3 2 1

Library of Congress Control Number 2016933376

ISBN 978-1-4814-8440-4

ISBN 978-1-4814-1415-9 (*Welcome Home!* eBook)

ISBN 978-1-4814-1418-0 (*Buttercup Mystery* eBook)

ISBN 978-1-4814-1421-0 (*Runaway Pony* eBook)

ISBN 978-1-4814-1424-1 (*Finding Luck* eBook)

These titles were previously published individually by Aladdin.

Contents

Welcome Home!

♥

*To my mom, who knows how to make
a place feel like home*

Chapter 1

"WILLA, PLEASE STOP KICKING MY SEAT."

"Sorry, I didn't mean to," Willa Dunlap said to her mom as she stretched to see out the window. She really didn't mean to kick the seat. But they had been in the car FOREVER, driving all the way from Chicago to Chincoteague Island in Virginia.

Now Willa was about to miss out on the

very best part. She turned and looked out the back. All she wanted was a peek at one of the Chincoteague ponies, running on the sandy beach. She thought if she saw one, it would be a sign that moving to the island and leaving her friends behind was worth it.

Willa tried to see past the houses and across the bay but couldn't spot a thing. It was too foggy.

"We're almost home," Mom announced. "It's coming up on the left."

Willa rolled her eyes, hoping to get the attention of her little brother, Ben. He didn't like it when Mom called the new house "home," either. They didn't live there *yet*. And, as far as Willa knew, no one had lived in the old gray house in a long time. Willa thought there was a good

reason. It didn't look very "homey" in pictures.

She glanced around at the houses along the narrow street. They looked like they had been built a long time ago, but they did have lots of new flowers in the front yards. The Dunlaps had never had a yard, just a balcony in their last apartment in Chicago.

One of the houses on the street had a giant tree with a rope swing hanging from a high branch. Willa had only swung on the chain-link swings in the city parks with her best friend, Kate.

Ben had hardly said one word the whole ride. But that wasn't unusual for him. He had read through his comic collection and then napped. Willa couldn't nap. She couldn't even read one of the dozen books in her backpack. She was too anxious.

Their dad had been quiet too. He had been quiet a lot since they had decided to move. The only thing he had talked about was the new kitchen for the new restaurant they were going to open. Their parents were going to run a bed-and-breakfast, and their dad would be the head chef.

The whole family had agreed that they would call the restaurant the Family Farm. It sounded cozy and friendly. Dad liked how it hinted that they were going to try to grow some of their own food. Willa and Ben liked how it sounded as if there would be animals there. But neither Mom nor Dad had made any promises about pets.

"Yay! We're here! Our new home!" Mom made another happy announcement. Willa knew that, in many ways, this already was home for her mom. She had grown up on Chincoteague Island. She had grown up hearing the stories of the famous ponies of nearby Assateague Island.

Once the car was parked, Mom swung her door open, stepped out, and breathed in the seaside air. Willa could already smell the salt in the car. She remembered it from trips to her grandparents' house. The smell of the ocean was everywhere.

Willa jumped out of the backseat and joined her mother. She leaned back as she looked up to the roof and back down again. There was a lot of house to see: three stories; a big covered porch that wrapped around the front to the side; and lots of windows set on a sloping roof.

"You don't think it's haunted, do you?"

Willa flinched. She hadn't heard Ben come up behind her. It didn't help that he almost always spoke in a whisper.

"No," she answered, but the house was large

enough for a whole family of ghosts, plus grand-parent ghosts too. "It's just old. Mom and Dad will fix it up. You'll see."

Willa skipped to the end of the driveway and back, trying to loosen up her knees after the drive. Her parents stood in front of the house. Her dad had his hand resting on her mom's shoulder, and her mom had her arm around his waist.

"A cat!" Ben yelped.

He pointed and jogged up onto the porch. Wood planks creaked as he ran. The cat's fur was a mess of colors—brown, white, orange, and black—but its eyes were a clear, bright green.

Willa glanced at Dad and held her breath. How long until he tried to stop Ben? The cat's fur wasn't scraggly, and the animal wasn't terribly skinny, but it sure looked like a stray.

"Hey now, Ben," Dad called. "We don't know that cat."

Willa laughed. Of course they didn't know the cat.

"Don't get any ideas, buddy," Dad continued. "We have a lot of work to do around this place.

We cannot take on the responsibility of a pet right now."

What was the point of moving to a gigantic house if you couldn't have pets? Willa rushed to join Ben. She loved cats. She loved most animals. She understood what her dad was saying, but she hoped he would change his mind.

Just as Willa reached her brother, the cat jumped to the porch railing and began to lick her paw.

"I was so close," Ben said, his bangs hanging in his hazel eyes.

"Come on, you two," Dad called again. "We have to unpack this car. We don't have time to chase some stray cat."

"It isn't just any cat," a voice announced. "It's New Cat."

A barefoot kid in cutoff jeans stood in their driveway, holding a platter that was covered in shiny, silver foil. He didn't look much older than Ben.

"New Cat belongs here. She always has," the boy explained.

"Hi," Mom said. "I'm Amelia Dunlap. This is my family, Ben, Willa, and my husband, Eric."

"Hi," the boy answered, striding toward her. "I'm Chipper. My mom says, 'Welcome to Chincoteague.' She told me to give you these. You're lucky." He held out the platter. As soon as Willa and Ben's mom took it, the boy turned and ran.

Chapter 2

THE WHOLE FAMILY WATCHED CHIPPER RUN down the road.

Mom pulled back the foil from the casserole dish. "Oh, wow. Fried oysters! I'm sure of it." She breathed in the steam from the golden nuggets.

"We're going to eat *that*?" Willa asked.

Her mom nodded.

"But it's from a stranger," Ben pointed out. "You said to never eat food from strangers."

"There are no strangers on Chincoteague," their mom answered. She set the dish down on the porch stairs and took a seat. "Come on, you guys."

Their dad seemed even less sure about the mystery food. He leaned in to smell it for himself. "I'm not going to turn down homemade food," he said, "but I would rather be making dinner in my own kitchen." Willa and Ben locked eyes. There Dad went, talking about the new kitchen again.

"Oysters are seafood, aren't they?" Ben made a funny face.

"Turn up your nose all you want. It leaves more for me." Mom picked a crispy piece from

the dish. She dipped it into the creamy sauce and took a noisy bite. She closed her eyes. "Delicious," she said, reaching for another.

Dad grabbed the next-largest piece and popped it into his mouth. "I take it back," he said. "I will happily eat this over my cooking. It's fantastic."

It was not often that their dad enjoyed someone else's cooking. Sometimes a sandwich was "boring" or mashed potatoes were "too gummy." Dad had an odd way of talking about food.

Ben took a small bite. "I don't even taste the seafood," he admitted. "I don't even see the seafood." Ben cracked himself up.

The whole family took turns picking up the last crumbs of deep-fried goodness. In the open air, it felt like the start of a new adventure that they would all share. But for Willa, it changed as soon as they went inside.

The house was dusty and dim. The sun cast long shadows across the wooden floor. The ceilings were high and the rooms empty. There was a lot of space, but to Willa it didn't feel like home.

Willa's large duffel bag threw her off balance. She adjusted her grip as she started up the old, wide staircase.

"Honey, just leave everything in the main room for tonight," Mom said. "We need to clean the upstairs before we take stuff up there."

With a sigh, Willa dropped her backpack and duffel next to Ben's stuff. It didn't take her long to feel cooped up, surrounded by boxes and packed bags.

When Ben followed their parents to the back of the house, Willa slipped out the front door.

She could practically smell her way to the bay. The breeze swept in from the ocean. She followed the road they had driven on earlier until she came to a path. It was narrow and cut through the tall marsh grass.

When Willa and Ben had visited before, she had explored lots of paths with Grandma Edna, her mom's mom. Grandma Edna knew every path, every plant, and every family on Chincoteague.

Willa was surprised her grandparents hadn't

been at the house to greet them. She guessed they'd be over bright and early in the morning.

Grandma Edna and Grandpa Reed had come to see them in the city for holidays, but the Dunlaps hadn't been to visit them on the island in a few years. Spending more time with their grandparents was a good part of moving. Willa tried not to think about the bad ones.

Leaving her best friend, Kate, was one of them. What if Willa didn't make any friends here? What if it never felt like home?

The path finally led to a long dock that reached far into the water. Sitting down at the end, Willa felt just a little closer to Assateague, which was just across the bay.

Willa knew about the wild ponies there. Her mom had read her books, and Willa had

found others in the library. The most famous of
the ponies was Misty. Misty had been born on
Assateague, but she had ended up living with a
family on Chincoteague. That was a really long
time ago.

For a few months after she had read the
book about Misty, Willa had lived for ponies.
She had reread the books and taken horseback-

riding lessons. That was before the six months of ice-skating and the year of gymnastics. Willa had read a lot about those things too, until she had found something new.

But the ponies weren't like famous ice-skaters or gymnasts. The ponies were a mystery to Willa. They lived on their own, surviving on their instincts. Part of Willa still didn't believe their stories were true.

Willa took off her sandals and dangled her legs over the side. She gazed across the bay. She wondered if the ponies on the island felt free and if—

C-r-e-a-k-k-k . . .

Willa jumped as the dock creaked behind her.

"It's beautiful, isn't it?" her mother said, and sat next to Willa. Surprisingly, she was barefoot. Willa couldn't remember the last time she had seen her mom barefoot outdoors.

Willa nodded. "Is it really true?" she asked. "The story of the wild ponies?"

"Well, there isn't any way to prove it, but I believe it is true. I believe the old stories of the Spanish ship caught in a storm, and I believe that when the ship crashed, the ponies escaped as the ship sank.

"They swam to the island of Assateague that you see right there. They learned how to live and take care of themselves in a new place. They've been surviving ever since."

Willa glanced over at her mom. She had a faraway look in her eyes. She squeezed Willa's hand.

"Anyway, we do know that Misty's story was

true," Mom said. "Dad and I have even talked about calling the bed-and-breakfast Misty Inn, because people love that story. A lot of them visit the island to see where Misty lived."

"But I thought we were calling it the Family Farm," Willa said.

"Well, that's the name of the restaurant," Mom explained. "We'll have a different name for the inn." She paused.

"It's a good thing you were here, young lady," Mom said, pushing Willa's hair behind her ear. "Because otherwise you'd be in trouble, running off like that."

"I thought you wanted us to be able to run off. You said you wanted us to explore more. Isn't that why we left the city?"

"Well, yes and no," her mom responded.

"I do want those things for you, but I also want to know where you are. And you still need to watch your brother. You know, this move won't be as easy on him."

Does she think this is easy for me? Willa wondered.

"Ben has a harder time making friends and trying new things." Her mom tried to explain. "You're always finding new hobbies. It's easier for you."

Mom reached out and squeezed Willa's hand again.

Willa knew her parents were worried about Ben, but she didn't think he needed someone around all the time, acting like a babysitter.

"Come on," Mom said, standing up. "It's time to get back." Willa put on her shoes and followed her mother. "The moving truck comes with our furniture tomorrow. So we're just going to use our sleeping bags in the main room tonight. Your dad's making popcorn."

Popcorn was a family tradition. And a family sleepover sounded like fun. And tomorrow, the real adventure would begin. At least she hoped it would.

Chapter 3

WILLA OPENED HER EYES WITH A START.

Something didn't seem right.

She looked to one side. She could see her parents were both soundly sleeping in the dim morning light.

But when she turned to the other, Ben was gone. His sleeping bag was empty.

She quickly dressed, tugged her gym shoes

on, and hurried out the back door.

Where is he? Willa worried. *Mom and Dad will be so mad at me if anything happens to him.*

She was staring at the old barn. It was in the very back corner of the lot, half hidden by tall grass and ivy vines.

Willa raced to the tall double doors, which were cracked open, and stepped inside.

"Ben?" she called out. "Ben?"

"Here I am," she heard him say.

"Where?" Willa asked.

"Up here! In the hayloft," Ben answered.

She looked up and there was her brother, sitting on the edge of a platform, swinging his legs. It wasn't like her brother to go off on his own.

A knot was in Willa's stomach. What if Ben

fell? She tried to keep her voice steady.

"Ben, you have to come down. Now. We don't even know if it's safe up there."

Ben's smile turned into a frown. He hadn't thought about the hayloft being dangerous. He stood up and walked to the ladder. But when he looked down, he panicked.

"I'm not climbing down that ladder," he said. "It's too far."

"Well, you climbed *up*," Willa said angrily.

"How about that rope?" Ben said, pointing to a thick rope that hung down to the barn floor. "It looks easier than the ladder."

Willa walked over to the rope to check it out. It was a pulley system.

She pulled on it hard. It seemed pretty secure.

Ben looped one leg around the rope and kept one on the loft. His body swayed away from the platform and then . . . he lost his balance.

Ben tried to throw a leg out to grab at the loft, but he couldn't reach. He grabbed the rope harder. His knuckles grew white as he dangled in the air.

"I'm stuck," he cried. "It won't move."

Willa steadied the rope from the ground. "You have to slide down. Loosen up on the rope and ease yourself down."

"I can't," Ben whispered. His eyes were squeezed shut.

"You have to, or else you'll be hanging there all day. And I don't know if the pulley will hold that long."

Ben's hands burned as the old rope slid

through them. "Almost," Willa said. "You can just drop."

Ben paused but then let go, landing on his backside.

He stared at his hands. They were scraped and bloody, and they stung.

Ben bit his lower lip to keep from crying. He wiped his hands on the back of his pants.

Willa sat next to her brother and put her arm around his shoulder.

"You'll be okay," she said. "But next time, wake me up before you go."

From where they sat, Willa could see that the barn had different sections. "Stalls," she whispered happily to herself. Horses or ponies had probably lived there at one time. Of course, it was the *perfect* place for animals of all kinds.

Willa and Ben had never had pets in the city. Not even a fish.

Ben took a deep breath. "Is it my fault?" he said, looking up at the loft.

"What?" said Willa.

"Is it my fault that we had to move? The whole playground thing, with those older kids?"

"Don't be silly," Willa said. "Mom's wanted to move for years."

What Willa had said was true, but Ben had caught her off guard. He hadn't ever talked about the boys on the playground—the ones the teachers had warned his parents about. The ones who always teased Ben because he was so quiet.

"But Dad didn't want to move," Ben reminded

her. "Maybe he changed his mind because of me."

"Maybe he did," Willa admitted. "But it doesn't matter. We're here now."

Her words were drowned out by the sound of an engine. Willa stood up and rushed over to the barn door.

"It's Grandma and Grandpa," she called to her brother. "Come on."

Willa held her hand out to Ben, to help him stand, and they ran out to see their grandparents.

"There you are!" Grandma Edna said, opening her arms wide. Both Willa and Ben hurried over for a warm hug. She smelled sweet, like fresh hay. She wrapped one arm around each grandchild. "Can you believe we'll get to see them all the time now, Pops?"

"Nope. Still hasn't quite sunk in." Grandpa Reed waited patiently. The two kids snuggled in to him next.

"Hello!" The kids' parents waved from the porch. Mom rushed down the steps. She was already dressed in her old jeans and a long-sleeved plaid shirt. Her hair was pulled back in a low ponytail. Mom first hugged her mom. Next she leaned over Ben's head to kiss Grandpa Reed on the cheek.

"Look, there's the cat again," Ben exclaimed as he pointed to the back porch.

"Wait a minute, Ben. What happened to your hands?" Mom grabbed Ben's wrist and looked at his bloody palm.

"It's just a cut from a rope in the barn," Willa tried to explain. She gave Ben a *Don't say a word* look. Her mom glanced at the old building. "You'd better go wash those hands off."

"But the cat," Ben insisted.

"No way are you touching that cat with an open cut," Mom replied. "Eric, can you take Ben inside? The Band-Aids are in my bag."

They all watched them go inside. Grandma

Edna turned to her daughter. "You're going to need to loosen up a little, Amelia," she said. "Kids need room to breathe and solve their own problems."

"Mom, you know that's part of the reason we moved here," Mom huffed. Willa had never heard her mom and grandma argue.

"Now, you two," Grandpa Reed said after a pause. "You're both coming from the same place so don't fight. I'm coming from the place of hunger. Willa, why don't you give me a quick tour so we can head on inside and eat. Grandma made some of her strawberry scones."

Willa took her grandpa's hand. They walked toward the back of the house, and Grandma Edna followed. New Cat was right behind them. "I haven't had much time to explore yet," she confessed. "But I saw these beautiful flowers on the back fence."

Grandpa Reed looked up and nodded.

"Nasturtiums," Grandma Edna told them. "Why, they're just lovely."

"I could use those in salads." That was Dad again. He and Ben had returned. Ben had white gauze wrapped around his palms. "But we'll have to get a lawn mower to get anywhere close to them."

"Oh, a few goats could take care of that over-grown grass," Grandma suggested.

Eric coughed back a laugh. "We are starting a bed-and-breakfast, Edna, *not* a petting zoo."

Grandpa Reed broke in. "Yes, dear, we all know that you will find any excuse to surround yourself with more animals. But we all also know that it's time for breakfast." With that, he lifted Ben by the middle and swung him upside down. Ben giggled. "This boy's ready to eat. He's light as a feather. Let's plump him up."

Grandpa Reed led everyone inside. Willa walked behind. She liked the way her grandma thought. What was the point in having a big house and big yard if you didn't share it with animals? They needed at least one pet, maybe two. And the sooner the better.

Chapter 4

THEY HADN'T BEEN TO THEIR GRANDPARENTS' house in years, but Willa had warm memories of their little island farm. Grandma Edna, who was a veterinarian, ran a small animal rescue center. She had taken in everything from pet rabbits to geese to goats. And, of course, Chincoteague ponies.

"Remember how she let us throw flakes of

hay into the pony paddock last time?" Willa asked Ben in a whisper. Her brother nodded. "You were so small, you could hardly reach over the fence."

Willa and Ben were sitting in the backseat of their grandparents' truck, on the way to their farm. Once their bikes arrived, they'd be able to visit on their own, whenever they wanted.

Ben frowned as Willa giggled. A lot had changed, and he was definitely taller now. Maybe this time he'd get to ride a pony by himself.

"They still have ponies, right?"

"I think so," Willa answered. "Mom said that Grandma's getting older and isn't taking in new animals anymore. And there's another pony rescue on the island now too."

When they turned onto the long driveway to

Miller Farm, Ben saw his sister cross her fingers. He looked past her to the fenced-in field. There, a small band of ponies came into view. They weren't the silky sleek horses like at the riding stable near the city. These ponies had muddy knees and thick, shaggy manes. They were still beautiful.

Grandpa brought the truck to a stop close to a one-story house.

"You'll have to meet the newest member of our herd," Grandma said as she swung the passenger door closed. She motioned to a horse that was nearly twice as tall as the ponies. He was all black, except his legs had long white hair from the knee down. "Jake is a Shire, a real, live draft horse. He's a bigger sweetheart than the rest combined."

"Literally," Grandpa uttered, helping Ben and Willa jump down from the backseat of the truck.

"The ponies are all moving on in age," Grandma Edna explained, motioning to the field. "They're getting more stubborn by the day. They aren't much for riding anymore. Annie pins back her ears whenever she sees a saddle. Oh, she pins her ears all the time." Grandma pointed to a chestnut mare with a star on her forehead. Willa remembered that she had ridden Annie the last time she visited Miller Farm. Well, she'd sat on Annie, and Grandma had led her around.

"Truth is," Grandma continued, "I don't have time for riding either. But Jake loves to get out and about."

Willa sighed. While there were still ponies on the farm, it sounded like they were pretty much off limits. Except for Jake, and he was so tall, Willa couldn't imagine getting on him.

"Can I pet him?" Ben asked. The horse had eased his way to the fence.

When Grandma nodded, Ben stepped forward and held out his hand. The draft horse's great tongue licked Ben's fingers. Ben laughed.

"Jake's always friendly, but the ponies are only interested if you have a treat," Grandma explained.

"They're a hungry bunch," Grandpa said.

"No more than you, Reed. It's just their nature. They're grazers. It's their job, eating enough to keep them going.

"Come on, kids. We should water the horses,"

Grandma Edna said. It was a funny term, but Willa knew they weren't going to throw water on the horses. It meant filling up the drinking trough. Grandpa went inside to make sandwiches, and Willa helped Grandma untangle the green hose. She slid it through the fence and into the metal trough.

"Edna!" Grandpa called from the door. "Clifton left a note for you. Says a fellow named Worth called on the barn phone and is on his way over."

Grandma nodded as she worked the kinks out of the hissing hose. "Clifton's a teenager who helps out around the place," she said. "He's awful nice, and he's got a sister about your age, Willa."

Willa smiled, but she didn't have time to ask

questions. A truck and trailer began its way up the farm's long gravel drive. They all turned to look.

The truck stopped, and a man with a cowboy hat got out and shut the door. "You Edna Miller?" he asked.

"Well, yes."

"My name's Dale Worth. I got your name from a friend. She said you take in Chincoteague ponies."

Grandma opened her mouth to answer, but the man kept right on talking.

"My neighbors are going through a rough patch and need to let their pony go. I promised them I'd take care of it. So here I am, and here's the pony." He motioned to the battered trailer and moved toward its back end.

"I'm not exactly taking new animals," Grandma called out.

"I called earlier," Mr. Worth said, "but I've only got the trailer for the day, so I came ahead."

"Now's not the best time," Grandma continued. "The fence on our small paddock is broken. We have no way to separate a new animal from the herd."

The man kept moving as Grandma talked. He lifted a lever and pulled down a ramp.

Grandma had more to say, but the man disappeared inside the trailer. There was the shuffling of hooves on metal, and then a sleek buckskin backed down the ramp.

Willa held her breath. Ben's jaw dropped. Grandma Edna just stared.

The pony snorted as she stood next to Mr. Worth. Her ears twitched. Her coat was a creamy butterscotch, and her mane and tail were the color of cocoa. Her dark eyes were warm and friendly.

"This here's Starbuck," Mr. Worth said. "She's a nice mare, but she loved her owner. I suspect she's going to be lonesome not having young Merry around."

Ben looked at Grandma. Her eyes were steady on the pony, but it looked like she had all kinds of thoughts churning around in her head.

Willa couldn't understand why Grandma wasn't running up and hugging the pony that very second.

"She looks to be a fine horse," Grandma said, "but I don't have the paddock space now. Like I said, my other gate's broken."

Ben had heard Mom describe Grandma as "being stubborn as a mule." Why was the broken fence such a big problem?

"I can't come back. My place is more than an hour south of here, and this pony needs a home now," Mr. Worth explained.

Willa felt a tightness across her chest.

She looked at Grandma. Why was she taking so long?

Finally Grandma spoke. "Where are the papers?" she asked.

Mr. Worth hesitated. "I don't have them, but the family promised they'd send the paperwork as soon as things settle."

"This is very unusual," Grandma said, shaking her head. "Very unusual."

She took a deep breath. For the first time, her eyes looked over to her grandchildren. "What do you think, should we take this pony?"

Ben's eyes grew in size. Willa could barely speak but managed to say, "It seems like the right thing to do."

"Yes," Ben agreed.

"Very well," Grandma concluded. "I suppose

we could clear out a space in the barn for the time being." She took the pony's lead and handed it to Willa while she got contact information from Mr. Worth.

Even in the hot summer sun, Willa had goose bumps. She reached out and smoothed the soft hair along the mare's neck. Ben picked a long blade of grass. He let Starbuck eat it from his hand.

They were still standing there when Mr. Worth backed the truck and trailer down the drive. They were both smiling.

Chapter 5

"EDNA?"

Willa and Ben turned when Grandpa called.

"She's in the barn," Ben said.

"She said she has to figure out which stall Starbuck will go in," Willa explained.

"Starbuck?" Grandpa asked, his eyes lingering on the new pony. "Edna?" he called again.

At that moment Grandma came out of the

barn, but she didn't see Grandpa. She had a bucket of brushes in one hand and a flake of hay in the other.

"I need one of you to help move some feed bags. The other can help me groom the mare, make her feel at home. Remember how we did it when you last visited?" She stopped short when she saw Grandpa.

"I go in the house for five minutes and there's a new horse in our driveway when I come out?" He tried to hide a stubborn smile.

"It must be what Clifton's note was about. This pony needs a place to stay for a while, until I can find her a better home," Grandma explained.

"I've heard that before," said Grandpa.

"Well, I thought the timing might be right,"

Grandma replied. She raised her eyebrows and tilted her head toward Willa and Ben.

Grandpa laughed. "Your grandma might be retired," he said, "but animals still run her life."

"They keep finding me," Grandma admitted.

While Grandpa helped Grandma in the barn, Ben and Willa took turns brushing Starbuck.

The pony didn't really need brushing. She didn't have a speck of dirt on her, but she seemed to like the attention. Willa ran the currycomb in circles on her belly, and Ben petted the swirl of hair on the center of her face. "What did Grandma mean when she said 'for a while'?" Ben asked.

"I don't know," Willa said with a shrug. "Mom said that Grandma sometimes finds a

new home for the animals, the ones that don't really need to be at a rescue center."

Starbuck let out a deep sigh. So did Willa. The pony turned around to give her shirt a friendly nip. "I know, girl," Willa said. "I sure hope you get to stay here."

♥

When it was time to introduce Starbuck to her stall, the pony didn't want to budge. "Move on," Grandma said, patting the pony on the rump.

Starbuck stepped forward with slow, stiff movements. Ben walked next to Grandma, carrying the brushes. "Looks like it hurts her," he said.

Grandma looked down. "I think you're right, Ben."

They took the pony to her stall for a closer look.

"See how nice this stall is?" Willa said as she led Starbuck inside. The stall smelled of fresh sawdust.

Grandma knelt by the mare's side. She ran her hands down her leg. "Sure enough," Grandma said, "she's got heat and swelling in this leg. It could be from the trailer ride, or maybe from before. It's a good thing we have a place to keep her. I don't think she'll be ready for the paddock for a while."

Grandma told Willa and Ben that the leg wasn't too bad. "But she'll need company so she doesn't get bored in this stall. It's no fun to be cooped up on your own, is it?" Grandma scratched Starbuck on her lower lip.

"We're happy to help," Willa said eagerly.

Ben nodded. He petted the pony's muzzle, which was the softest thing he had ever felt.

Every morning Willa and Ben rode their bikes to their grandparents' farm. They did whatever chores Grandma Edna gave them—weeding the garden, cleaning the saddles, sweeping the barn. But she did warn her grandchildren. "We don't know much about this pony," she told them. "For now, no going in her stall unless I am in the barn too."

Mom and Dad were so busy with the house—the furniture had arrived and the rooms needed to be set up—that they didn't have time to take the kids around to all the local sights. "The carpenters are coming on Saturday," Mom said. "We have a lot to figure out before they arrive."

But Ben and Willa didn't care. Even though they hadn't seen or met any kids their own age—except for Chipper—they had each other.

And for once, they wanted to do the exact same thing: see Starbuck. Willa couldn't believe that for the past few days, she hadn't thought about Chicago or Kate once. She had Starbuck to thank.

Chapter 6

ONE MORNING, THE SMELL OF BANANA BREAD
woke both kids and they hurried downstairs.
They had been on the island almost a week, and
this was the first homemade breakfast. "This is
really good, Mom," Willa said. Their dad was a
chef, but Mom was the baker.

"I need you two to do me a favor." Mom was
holding a casserole dish with an envelope taped

inside. "We need to return this. I did some detective work, and Chipper is one of the Starling kids. They also have an older girl. They live up the road."

By "detective work," Willa knew that her mom had talked to Grandma Edna. They hadn't seen Chipper since that first night. And now Mom probably wanted them to make friends with the Starling kids.

"Do I have to go too?" Ben asked.

"Yes, you do," Mom said. "I hear that the Starlings have something new in their backyard that you'll be interested in."

When they were a few yards from the porch, Mom opened the door. "I invited them to a picnic at our house," she called out. "After the construction's done. Just so you know."

Willa smiled at Ben. Mom *loved* picnics. Even though they had a huge house now, she would rather plan a gathering outside.

"I wonder what the surprise is," Willa said, gripping the dish in both hands. "Maybe a trampoline."

"Or a pool," Ben offered.

When they came to the house, Willa realized it was one she had noticed when they first moved in. There was a swing hanging from a large tree, bikes on the lawn, and wildflowers.

The doorbell was under a hand-painted plaque with the words, WELCOME TO OUR HOUSE. HOPE YOU FEEL AT HOME. Willa pushed the bell and waited. A happy scream came from the backyard. "Maybe it *is* a pool," Willa whispered.

The door opened. A woman who was not much taller than Willa greeted them. She had short almond-brown hair and big blue-rimmed glasses that made her look like a librarian in an old book.

"We're returning this," Willa said. She handed the dish over.

"You must be the Dunlaps," the woman said. "Willa and Ben, right? Your grandma has told me all about you. Sorry my kids haven't been over. They've been busy. I can't get them to leave the backyard."

"It's okay," Willa said. "We've been busy too. Thank you for the oysters. They were delicious."

"My dad would really like the recipe," added Ben.

"Ben," Willa said, "you can't just ask some-one for the recipe."

"Well," Mrs. Starling said, taking the dish in her hands. "I'll have to think about that. It is an old family secret." She smiled like a helpful librarian too.

Willa and Ben followed her through the house. Books and wooden ducks were every-where. When they came to a sliding glass door, she opened it. "Chipper! Sarah! The Dunlaps are here."

Two kids looked up from where they sat on a plaid blanket. Ben looked at Willa—it definitely was not a pool.

"Why don't you show them the puppies?" Mrs. Starling said. "Just keep it down. Bess is napping," she reminded them.

"Bess is our little sister," Chipper explained once Willa and Ben reached the blanket. "We have a big sister too. Kat."

"Katherine," Sarah corrected. She smoothed out her dark shiny hair, then her skirt. "We just got Marnie about a couple of months ago," she continued. "We didn't know she was pregnant."

Chipper pointed to the black and white pups. "That's Amos, Ranker, Bella, Dolly, Rice Cake, Tramp, and Jubilee," he said, rattling off their names.

"They were born just before you moved in," he added. "They'll stay with Marnie for a few months. But then we have to give them away."

"All but one," Sarah added.

Ben reached out to lift Rice Cake, but the puppy squirmed and Ben dropped him.

"What did you just do?" Sarah cried. "You could have hurt him!"

Willa looked at her brother. His eyes filled with tears.

"It was a mistake," she said to Sarah. "He didn't mean to hurt Rice Cake."

Sarah frowned. "I think you should leave. *Now*."

Willa and Ben quickly stood up and turned to go. But Chipper stopped them.

"I have to bring my father his lunch," he said. "Want to come along for the ride?"

"Sure," answered Willa. She and Ben turned to go back into the house, but Chipper headed to the other side of the yard, toward a long wooden walkway that led to a short dock.

"We're taking a boat?" she asked.

"It's just a skiff. It's okay," Chipper said. "I'm a good driver." Chipper handed them life jackets and leaned down to untie the boat.

Once she was buckled, Willa stepped into the front of the skiff. Her whole body wavered as the boat sloshed underneath her. She quickly sat down. "Hold on tightly, Ben," Willa warned her brother.

Ben watched his sister from the dock. He fiddled with his straps. Ben wondered if this was allowed. What would Mom say? They were getting in a boat with a stranger—and that stranger was a kid! Chipper finished untying the boat.

Ben glanced at his sister's back, took a deep breath, and stepped in.

"My dad's a fisherman," Chipper said, once they were on their way. "He takes people on fishing cruises. We've got to get there before they leave." As the motor revved, the front of the small boat lifted out of the water. Willa grabbed on to her seat. The boat made its way out of a small creek into the open bay.

"So, you probably know that Assateague is over there, with the wild ponies," Chipper told them after a while. "And this is about where the ponies come across on swim day."

Willa and Ben both looked from one shore to the other. The white sands of Assateague looked far from the marshy banks of Chincoteague. The ponies swam it every year, even the new colts. Then many of the youngest ponies would go up to auction the next day. It was how Chincoteague's Volunteer Fire Department kept track of the herd. They needed to keep it from getting too big. Assateague was a small island. Only so many ponies could live there.

Willa couldn't help thinking of Starbuck. Ben couldn't either. Mr. Worth had said she was a *real* Chincoteague pony. Had she swum the full length of the bay when she was a foal? What was her story?

Had Starbuck been born on Assateague, as wild as the sea?

Willa let the salty air fill her lungs. She decided it was okay if Sarah didn't want to be friends. Her brother, Chipper, still seemed nice.

But he would be a better friend for Ben than for her.

Willa clung to the hope that Grandma wouldn't find a home for Starbuck. As long as she could be with Starbuck, she could be happy. Still, she knew it wasn't the same as having a friend. She tried pushing that thought out of her head, but it stayed with her all the way to dropping off lunch, and even after she and Ben returned home to Misty Inn.

Chapter 7

Dear Kate,

I miss you so, so, so much.

How is camp? Tell me some of the new stuff you learned on the computer.

It is so different here in Chincoteague. This morning chickens woke Ben and me up.

Then this woman, Mrs. Cornett, who was wearing red boots and a yellow poncho, came out of nowhere and said they were hers. We did help her bring her chickens home, but how strange is that?

I've only met one girl, and we are already not friends.

My grandma and grandpa have a really nice farm with lots of horses. Ben and I go there every day, and we're taking care of a pony named Starbuck.

My parents still won't let us have a pet, but there is a cat here.

I've decided that Ben and I are going to try to make a fort in the barn that's in the back of our house. There's a lot of gross, old stuff in it, like rusty coffee cans, but I did find a bowl that says "Woof" in the bottom.

I sure wish you were here with me to help us build it.

Love,

Willa

Chapter 8

EARLY EVERY MORNING WILLA AND BEN WOULD go to the barn and spend time building their fort. They had already cleaned up the hayloft and thrown out a huge pile of junk.

But they couldn't wait to see Starbuck each day. And she seemed pleased to see them.

The buckskin pony had grown used to them. Grandma Edna had noticed. She now allowed her grandchildren to go in and out of Starbuck's stall as if the pony were their own.

One day Grandma had a surprise for Willa and Ben when they arrived at the farm.

"You've both been working hard. It's about time you got to take a ride," she said. In a few minutes, they were both saddled up.

Willa was in front on Maude, a steady pinto. Ben was on the great Jake. Grandma Edna walked on foot, staying close by Ben's side.

"He's like a big easy chair," Grandma said, glancing up at Ben. "You can't fall off. He's too wide."

As Ben eased forward and back with Jake's every step, he thought it was closer to sitting in a rocking chair—a rocking chair on the beach. From Jake's back, Ben had a fine view of the farm. He could almost see out to the ocean.

"Isn't it windy on Assateague?" Ben asked. "What about winter? Don't the horses get cold?"

Grandma Edna paused. "Well, yes, I'm sure they do. But those ponies are tough. They've learned to take care of themselves. And nature gives them heavier coats when it gets cold."

"I don't think Starbuck would do so well over there," Ben said.

"Well, she's been pampered," Grandma replied. "She probably had a heavier coat in the winter, but her old owner groomed it away in spring. And you and Willa have brushed that pony to no end."

It was true. When they weren't wrapping

her leg or adding fresh sawdust to her stall, they had a mane comb, currycomb, or brisk brush in hand. Starbuck loved the attention. She would turn her head and watch Willa and Ben with her warm brown eyes.

"Starbuck is the best friend we've made, Grandma. We need to take care of her." Ben sounded sincere.

Willa turned around in her saddle again. Sometimes Ben surprised her. "I think you're right," Willa said. "Grandma, why do you think her old owner gave up Starbuck?"

"I'm not really sure, honey. Mr. Worth said we'd get more information soon. When we do, I'll let you know," Grandma answered.

Back at the barn, Starbuck was waiting for them. She nickered a low greeting when Willa and Ben carried in their saddles. "I wonder if we'll ever get to ride *her*," Ben said, almost to himself.

"It depends," Willa said. "Grandma might still be looking for another home for her. And she doesn't want us to grow too attached."

"But we're already attached, Willa," said Ben.

At that moment Grandma came into the barn and hung up Jake's oversize bridle next to the much smaller ones that fit the ponies. "I'm a little worried about your girl, Starbuck. She needs to get outside, but she's not ready to be in the paddock. The other horses have been together for a long time. They are not always friendly with newcomers."

Grandma had already explained to them that they used to have two paddocks. With two spaces, a new horse could go in one, and the older horses would stay in the other. They could slowly get used to one another. There were always one or two horses that liked to be in charge, and they would want to show the new horse who was boss. Grandma called it "herd dynamics."

"She needs fresh air," Grandma said, leaning down to run her hand over Starbuck's sore leg. "She's almost mended. Can't keep her cooped up much longer. Maybe you two could take her out for some grass?"

It felt like a whole new world, getting to take Starbuck out of the stall. They took her for a short walk along the far edge of the farm. The pony drew in deep breaths of air, her nostrils quivering. As pretty as she was in the barn, she seemed even more beautiful out in the open.

At Grandma's advice, they did not go far. They found a good patch of grass near the paddock fence and Starbuck happily ate.

All at once, the pony lifted her head. Her ears pricked toward a faraway sound. She called out in a high whinny.

From the far corner of the pasture, Annie's head rose. The older mare's ears pressed back against her neck. Starbuck neighed again. Annie's eyes flashed white with anger. She stretched out her neck and began to charge. She pounded across the grassy paddock, aiming right for Starbuck!

Ben scrambled up from the ground where he was sitting. Willa gripped Starbuck's halter and backed her away.

Annie's hooves skidded in the dirt when she reached the high fence. She snorted, her teeth bared.

"That's not very nice," Willa scolded the older pony. Starbuck stood behind her, rubbing her head against Willa's back. "We should probably find someplace else."

Annie stayed by the fence, eyeing the newcomer. "I don't like the way she looks at Starbuck," Ben said. He scrunched up his face at the chestnut pony.

Willa tugged at the lead line, but Starbuck wouldn't move. Even though the pony turned her head toward Willa, her hooves stayed put. "She doesn't want to go," Ben said.

"She's got to. She can't stay here," Willa said.

Ben rubbed his lips together, looking at the

pony's warm eyes and alert ears. He walked over and leaned against Starbuck's backside, giving her a nudge. "It's okay, girl," he murmured.

The three of them headed toward the barn. Grandma helped put Starbuck back in her stall and then asked, "How would you both like to get some ice cream?"

Ben and Willa piled in the backseat of the truck. Willa wondered if the ice cream on Chincoteague was as good as the ice cream at Blue Hills in Chicago.

When they pulled up to the stand, Willa didn't want to get out of the truck.

Sarah Starling and her little sister, Bess, were there with their mother.

"Come on, Willa," Grandma said. "There's a long line and I'm hungry."

She smiled.

Grandma and Mrs. Starling said hello and talked about the upcoming Dunlap picnic. But Sarah didn't say *one* word to Willa—or to Ben. She just glared at them and played with the seam on her skirt. Luckily, it was not long before she left with her sister and mother.

Ben ordered a double scoop of chocolate, Grandma had butter pecan, and Willa had strawberry with sprinkles. The ice cream was yummy, but it didn't keep Willa from feeling a little bit sick to her stomach: What was going to happen when Sarah and her entire family came to the Dunlaps' next week? It could only be disaster.

Chapter 9

THE NEXT MORNING WILLA COULD HARDLY MOVE.

"Why am I so sore?" Willa complained to her mother. "I've ridden horses before." She squatted down, then stood up and shook out her legs.

"Your muscles aren't used to it. It's been a long time since you took lessons," Mom reminded Willa. She paused and looked at the measuring tape. They were in the third-floor bedroom. It was going to be part of the bed-and-breakfast, and the windows needed new curtains. Willa held one end of the tape to the corner of the window frame.

Her mom was right. It had been a long time since she had taken lessons. Willa wondered what it would be like if she hadn't given up horseback riding. She had learned a lot in the months she had taken lessons in Chicago. She knew how to be calm around horses, how to brush in the direction that the hair grew, and how to place her hand on a horse's side or rump to let it know where she was in the stall. The riding trainer had taught her all those things.

Between leg stretches, Mom asked, "Wasn't

Four Corners the best ice cream you've ever had? How was Ben when you were there? Did he say much?"

Of course Mom was more concerned about Ben. He still didn't say much, but that was Ben.

Before Willa could answer Mom's question, or tell her about mean Sarah Starling, a loud howl came from downstairs.

"It's Dad," Willa said. "It sounds like he's in pain." They dropped the tape and raced down the stairs, to the kitchen.

"Are you okay?" gasped Mom.

Dad was standing in the center of the room holding a broom over his head. He was slowly turning in circles, his gaze on the ground. Ben was sitting on the new wooden counter. He was as quiet as ever but had a huge smile on his face.

Without looking up, Dad said, "I saw a mouse. No, not just one. Two."

"Mice," Ben said.

A sigh of relief came from Mom. "You screamed so loud. I thought you'd cut off your hand!" Mom started laughing.

Dad was still spinning around. He was now holding the broom like a hatchet. "This isn't funny," he declared.

"We've had mice before," Willa pointed out. "We had them every spring in the city."

"But that was in our home," Dad reminded them. "This is also supposed to be a restaurant. The health inspectors will never approve a kitchen with mice!" Dad said.

"Traps never work, and I refuse to put out poison."

"Well, there is a simple solution," Mom began.

Listening to Mom, Ben's eyes grew wide.

Willa's heart bounced. Was Mom saying what they thought she was saying?

"All right." Dad gave in. "Go find that cat."

New Cat proved to be a good mouser. They never saw her actually catch a mouse, but she was always sniffing around the kitchen and standing guard. She would stare at the cabinets for hours, tail swishing, and would not leave her post. It took only a couple of days and the mice were gone.

"It's like all the mice packed up and left once they realized she was here," Dad said.

"They'll leave if they smell a cat," Mom said. "There are plenty of other, safer places for a mouse family to live around here."

Dad reached down and gave New Cat a

stroke from head to tail. "I appreciate a pet that can earn its keep."

Ben and Willa appreciated New Cat too. She was their first real pet, after all. Early on, the cat did not leave the kitchen. But after a couple of days—and no more signs of mice— she wandered into the family room.

Ben liked to scratch her under the chin, where her creamy white fur was soft. Willa gave her pets along the back. When New Cat was off duty, she enjoyed napping in a sunny window.

Every morning she would follow Willa and Ben to the barn, and watch them clean and sweep and move hay from one end of the space to the other. Even though they would have loved a horse, New Cat was a nice start.

Chapter 10

WILLA THOUGHT THAT TIME MOVED MORE slowly on Chincoteague. But before she knew it, it was the Friday of the family picnic. The Dunlaps were in the kitchen bright and early. Willa was helping Dad with the potato salad. Ben was helping Mom with the sugar cookies.

Mom seemed nervous.

"The first party in a new house is never

easy," she said, her head inside the pantry.

"It's not just a new house," Dad added, chopping a celery stalk. "It's also a new kitchen."

It was a new kitchen, but the fancy new stove did not fit in its space between the cabinets. The dishwasher was still in the box, so there was lots of dish and glass washing every day.

At around eleven, Mom told the kids, "Your dad and I have a lot to do. Maybe you want to ride your bikes to your grandparents' for a while? But please be home by three to help set up."

As they neared Miller Farm, they heard a high, shrill whinny. Another followed it. "Starbuck!" Willa called out. They were still at the bottom of the gravel driveway. They couldn't see the paddock. A third whinny rang out. The cry didn't sound like it could come from the calm mare with the soft brown eyes, but Ben agreed with Willa. He was sure it was Starbuck too.

Willa reached the top of the driveway first. Ben threw down his bike and ran to catch up with her. They joined Grandpa, who was already at the paddock gate. They all looked to the far side of the pasture to where Starbuck and Annie were facing off.

"What happened?" Willa asked.

"Well, I let Starbuck out," Grandpa said. "She was kicking in her stall. I thought she'd knock the barn down. Seemed like the best thing was to let her stretch her legs."

"But she was hurt, Grandpa," Willa said.

"Your grandma said she was better. I just

assumed that meant she was all right for the pasture."

Ben gripped the fence. He was listening, but he didn't take his eyes off the ponies. Starbuck's eyes flashed and her nostrils flared. There had to be something he could do.

"Where is Grandma?" Willa asked, looking around hopefully.

"Went into town. Had to go shopping before your folks' picnic." Grandpa took a handkerchief from his back pocket. He wiped his forehead.

Willa turned back to the paddock. Annie and Starbuck both had their ears pinned back. Annie took a step forward and stuck her neck out, her teeth bared. Starbuck stood her ground. "We have to get her out of there," Willa insisted. "Who knows what Annie will do."

"Annie's trying to show Starbuck who's boss," Grandpa said. "I think I know how to distract her. Annie doesn't think with her head. She thinks with her stomach.

"Willa, you come with me. Bring that pail. Ben, you keep watch," Grandpa directed. "Call us if they get any closer. Got it, bud?"

Ben nodded, his hands still tight on the

fence. Grandpa and Willa jogged toward the back of the house.

Annie inched forward, kicking up dust. The other horses kept their distance. Even Jake stayed near the gate. Starbuck didn't bare her teeth, but she also didn't back down. Annie came at her from the side and nipped her neck.

Starbuck squealed. Annie stamped and tried to back her into the fence. Starbuck skidded away. When Annie lunged, Starbuck swung around to face the older pony again. Starbuck's front leg shot up and she slammed her hoof to the ground.

"Leave her alone," Ben called out. He let go of the fence. "Get away! Starbuck didn't do any-thing." He heard muffled yells from Grandpa and Willa behind him, but he didn't care. Before

Ben knew it, he had unlatched the paddock gate and was walking quickly toward the two mares.

"No, you don't," Grandpa huffed, and rushed forward. He grabbed Ben by the arm. "You can't go in there, not with the horses acting like that." Grandpa tugged Ben out of the paddock. Willa locked the gate.

"But she won't leave Starbuck alone!" Ben looked at the ponies again. Their eyes were still fierce and their ears were still pinned. "She didn't do anything," he said, starting to cry.

"Don't you worry. We can get her out of there," Grandpa said, leaning down and looking Ben square in the eye. "But we have to get Annie away first. I made the mistake. I shouldn't have put Starbuck out there yet. The horses need more time to figure it out."

He stood up, his hand resting on Ben's back. "If you want to help her, how about you and Willa get that grouch Annie to take some carrots." Grandpa pointed Ben in the right direction and put a few carrots in his hands.

It was as easy as Grandpa said it would be. Annie lost all interest in Starbuck when she saw the fresh carrots dangled over the fence. The chestnut mare's ears pricked forward, and she didn't look like a cranky bully anymore.

She walked toward the kids. They carefully held out the carrots, one at a time, and Grandpa led Starbuck from the paddock. Then he locked the gate.

By the time Grandma came home, everything was back to normal. She was upset at first, but then put Grandpa to work right away, fixing the fence for the second field. That field would not only give Starbuck a place to graze, but it would let her get to know the other horses before they shared a paddock.

Willa and Ben let Starbuck eat grass behind the barn until the sun was high in the sky. Even then, it was hard putting her back in the stall.

"Grandpa's still working on the fence," Willa said. "When he's done, Starbuck can stay outside all she wants."

Willa turned to Ben and looked him in the eye. "You have to promise me you won't do anything like that again. I know you can take care of yourself, but you have to remember we're a team. We need to look out for each other."

"I know, Willa. I know," Ben said, and he meant it.

Chapter 11

"ARE YOU OKAY?" MOM ASKED, HUGGING BOTH Ben and Willa as they got out of their grandparents' truck. She grasped Ben by both shoulders. "What were you thinking?"

All the way home, sitting in the back of her grandparents' truck, Willa worried what her parents would do. They already knew about the paddock incident. Grandpa had called as soon as everyone was safe and sound.

"Amelia, your dad and I have already talked to them," Grandma explained. "Ben especially understands that he has to use his head around horses. Don't you?"

Ben nodded. He pressed his lips together. His parents were both looking at him with concern.

"I had to do it," Ben blurted. "I didn't want to stand there and watch Annie push Starbuck around. Annie was being mean. I just wanted to help Starbuck."

Now the whole family was looking at Ben in a new way.

"I understand why it was wrong. It was dangerous," he said, his words steady and clear. "I won't do it again."

Mom swept her hand over Ben's head and pulled him close. "I know," she said. "That pony is lucky to have you looking out for her."

"The kids are good with the new pony," Grandma said after a moment. "They've still got a lot to learn, but she trusts them." She smiled at Willa, who was holding Dad's hand. "Starbuck will be just fine. It takes time to get used to a new place and new horses."

They all seemed to take a deep breath, and then Dad looked around. "Speaking of new places, we're about to have company. We still have lots to do."

Ben carried two loaves of strawberry bread from Grandma's car. Willa helped her mom spread a tablecloth on the floor of the deck. "We still need outdoor furniture, but this will work for now," Mom said.

When Mom and Dad and the house were just about ready, Grandma called to Willa and Ben. "Come to the front porch," she said. The kids followed, and she handed a letter to Willa. "This came today in the mail."

As Willa pulled out the letter and started reading aloud, she realized it was from Starbuck's former owner.

Dear Mrs. Miller,

Thank you for taking care of my Starbuck. Mr. Worth told me that you seem exceptionally nice and that Starbuck will be happy on your farm. Sorry I didn't come to drop her off. It was hard for me. My family's moving for my dad's job, and Starbuck can't come. It won't feel like home without her.

I've sent her papers. She's a real Chincoteague pony. We got her at the auction when I was eight. I don't have any proof, but I like to think she could be related to Misty. You know, the pony from the famous book? When Starbuck raises her head and the wind blows through her mane, she looks like real royalty.

Please take care of Starbuck. She loves to be outside, get brushed, and be ridden bareback.

Maybe someday I can come back and
visit her.

   With kind thanks,

   Merry Meadows

Next, they unfolded the certificate and let it all sink in. Starbuck was a *real* Chincoteague pony, born in the wild on Assateague.

After a few moments of quiet, Willa carefully folded the papers and slid them back in the envelope.

Willa had never seen Ben look so happy. Ben had never seen his sister look so happy.

"I'll bet Grandma will never give her away now," Ben said.

"I hope you're right," Willa answered.

♥

The hens, although not invited, were the first to arrive. They squawked as they made their way to the back corner of the yard.

Next, Mrs. Starling peeked around the corner with her blue-rimmed glasses. Mr. Starling came close behind. Bess was on his back.

"Hey! Where's Ben?" Chipper called out. He was still barefoot, but he was far less shy than when they met him the first day. Sarah and their big sister, Katherine, were several steps away.

"Hello!" Mom said, getting up. "Thanks so much for coming."

Mrs. Starling was carrying the same casserole dish that the oysters had been in. "Let's get that to the kitchen," Mom said. "It's time to eat!"

There was a full spread on the island in the kitchen. Mrs. Cornett, the owner of the chickens, brought egg salad and deviled eggs. There was a fresh platter of Mrs. Starling's fried oysters. Dad pulled a big batch of macaroni and cheese from the oven.

"Did you get the new stove to fit?" Grandpa asked, looking around at the changes.

"No," confessed Dad, "but this old one is pretty good. We'll keep it until it conks out. Maybe we don't need a new one after all. We'll see when the inn opens in September."

People spread out to eat—some outside on the deck. Inside, guests sat at the long table.

The kids all sat together and ate faster than the adults. Chipper was telling Ben about the puppies, but Sarah paid more attention to her potato salad than she did to Willa.

When Ben was done eating, he asked Chipper, "Want to go in the barn? Willa and I are making it into a fort."

Willa followed the boys, and once they were in the barn, Chipper and Ben were knee deep in the straw pile. Willa climbed up to the hayloft and opened up the wooden window. She was thinking about Starbuck and how much she still missed Kate when she heard someone climbing up the ladder.

It was *Sarah*!

"This could be an awesome fort," she said quietly.

Willa couldn't believe Sarah was talking to her. She especially couldn't believe Sarah had climbed the old ladder in her sundress.

"You know, Willa," Sarah continued, "I'm sorry I wasn't very nice to you the first day. And then when we saw you at Four Corners."

Sarah sat down next to Willa. At first she didn't say anything, and then she said, "There was another family that lived here for a while before you. They were from the city too. There was a girl our age." She paused and looked up at Willa, then focused on her hands again. "They only lived here for a month before heading back. I thought you all would leave too."

At once, Willa realized what Sarah was saying. Building a friendship would take trust and time. "If you're worried that we're going to move, don't be. My parents just ordered the sign for the bed-and-breakfast, and my

grandparents are here," Willa explained. She counted the reasons why they would stay on her fingers. "My mom's going to help me plant a bunch of herbs soon, and we've adopted New Cat. We're not going anywhere. And," she said, "we just found out that a new pony at my grandma's is a *real* Chincoteague pony! Just like Misty!"

"Really?" Sarah asked. "That's awesome, Willa. Do you think I can go with you one day?"

Willa nodded. "Maybe tomorrow. I'll have to ask my grandma."

Things were slowly starting to come together.

"Hey, Ben. Chipper. Come on up to the loft. You have to see this!" she called down.

The boys climbed up, and all four kids gazed out the loft window, which looked out to the bay.

Down in the yard, Bess Starling was chasing New Cat.

New Cat was chasing Mrs. Cornett's chickens.

Mrs. Cornett's chickens were chasing one another.

All the adults were eating dessert and laughing.

Chipper yelled out, "Save some cake for me."

Then he looked over at Willa and Ben and said, "I'm glad you guys moved here."

And for the first time since they arrived in Chincoteague, Willa and Ben felt exactly the same way.

Buttercup Mystery

♥

To Olivia, Sophie, and Riley Kate

Chapter 1

"HEY, YOU GUYS IN THERE?"

Willa looked at her brother, Ben. "It's Chipper," she whispered. "You want to do it?"

Ben looked at the bucket above the door. The bucket was half full of water. A string was tied to its handle. The string was in Ben's hand. He had been using it to play with New Cat.

Ben chewed his lip. Chipper Starling was

his new best friend. Ben and Willa had lived on Chincoteague Island for only a few weeks. Ben thought for a few seconds and nodded at Willa.

"Yeah, we're here, Chipper. Come on in." Willa was at the back of the barn, out of the way.

As soon as Chipper poked his head in the tall double doors, Ben gave a yank. It could not have worked better. The water fell on Chipper, the bucket fell on the ground, and laughter filled the air.

"Got you back," Ben said.

"That was a good one." Chipper wrung out his shirt. New Cat, who also got wet, was licking the unwanted water from her fur.

"Nice job!" Willa gave Ben a high five. Chipper did the same.

Willa smiled when she saw the two boys

laughing. She was glad her brother had found a friend who shared his sense of humor. Even better, Chipper had a sister. His sister was the same age as Willa, and she loved horses and other animals. How lucky could Willa get?

It was funny, because Willa had not felt lucky when they had first moved. She had missed Chicago and her friends. She had not known if Chincoteague, with all its sand and salty air, could be home.

Even though their mom had grown up on the island, Willa and Ben had not spent much time in the little beach town. It was a big change for the whole family. They had left the city and a small apartment and now lived in a big Victorian house with three stories and a wraparound porch.

"You guys should come over to our place," Chipper said. A drip of water streamed from his forehead down his cheek. "Sarah wants to show you something, Willa. She sent me to tell you especially."

"Really? What is it?"

"I'm not allowed to tell." Chipper shrugged. "She was too excited, but she's stuck at home with Bess."

Bess was Sarah and Chipper's little sister. They had to watch her sometimes while their mom worked. Willa rested the broom in the corner. "You guys go ahead. I'll tell Mom and Dad." As she walked to the house, Willa tried to figure out what could be so exciting. Why wouldn't Sarah at least offer a hint? Willa could think of only one thing that was *that* exciting to her.

Willa watched her brother and Chipper shuffle down the drive, kicking up dust and sand on their way. She skipped up the porch steps and wiped the dirt off her freckled knees. "Mom, Dad?" she called. "I'm going over to Sarah's!" She headed down the hallway and, no surprise, found them both in the kitchen. Their old kitchen had room for only one person at a time, but this kitchen was four times that size. It needed to be. It would have to feed a lot more people when the family's bed-and-breakfast opened.

The Dunlaps had never run a hotel—or a restaurant—before. But Ben and Willa's dad had been a chef for years, and their mom liked a challenge. The family had agreed on Misty Inn as a name. Misty was a famous pony that had lived on Chincoteague long ago.

Willa glanced around the kitchen. It looked like Dad was already cooking for a whole hotel. Bowls of tomatoes, jars of spices, and mounds of chopped peppers covered the counter. "It's kind of early to be making dinner, isn't it?" Willa asked.

"He's trying out chili recipes," Mom said as Dad dumped some red powder into a steaming pot.

"I'm entering the Greater Chincoteague Chili Cook-Off," Dad explained. "And I plan to win it." He took a tiny taste from a large wooden spoon. "This is my second batch today."

Willa looked at the large clock above the stove. It wasn't even ten in the morning. "So, can we go to the Starlings'?" she asked. "Sarah has something to show me."

"Of course," Mom said. She smiled at Willa

from the other side of the laptop. "I'm just trying to find furniture for the guest bedrooms
today. Not very exciting."

Even though Mom said that, Willa knew her
mom loved that kind of stuff. In the new house,
Willa and Ben got their own bedrooms. Their
parents would share one, and then there were
three left over. The extra rooms would be for
guests, and Mom wanted the beds and dressers
to look old and stately.

Willa knew these things were fun for her parents. But she couldn't stay there another second. A surprise was waiting for her at the Starlings' house. But what?

"Wow, another horse?" Willa couldn't believe it. The Starlings already had one horse in their pasture, along with a couple of goats. Of course, a horse had been the one thing that Willa had thought of when Chipper said "exciting." Willa couldn't even imagine having one horse in her backyard, let alone two.

"Her name is Buttercup," Sarah said, rubbing the new horse's velvety muzzle. "Once she's settled in, Dad will use her for the pony swim and all that."

Sarah's dad was one of the island's saltwater

cowboys, which meant that he had the special job of helping with the roundups of the wild ponies on nearby Assateague.

From Chincoteague, Assateague looked like a little wisp of land before the great big open ocean. The small island was the home of two herds of wild ponies—ponies whose ancestors had escaped a stormy shipwreck hundreds of years before. They'd been taking care of themselves ever since.

Thinking about the wild ponies reminded Willa of Starbuck, the beautiful buckskin pony at her grandparents' nearby farm. Willa and Ben's grandma was a vet and had once run an animal rescue center on the island. Recently, a neighbor had left Starbuck at Miller Farm because the pony's owner could no longer care for her.

Willa and Ben were more than happy to look after Starbuck, but Grandma Edna felt that healthy animals did not need to be there. They needed to find new homes—forever homes.

"If your dad is going to use Buttercup for roundups, what about Sweetums?" Willa asked. She reached out to give the older horse a steady pat on his shiny black coat.

"That's the best part," Sarah said. "Dad knows how much I love Sweetums, so he's going to let me ride him more. He might even let me ride Sweetums in the carnival parade."

"No way!" Willa said. Chincoteague's Summer Extravaganza had rides, game booths, and tons of tasty food. The parade was on a Saturday morning and went straight through the town. It was for the local horses and pets, as well as some old cars and unicycles. Willa and Ben had heard all about the silly costumes people wore. It sounded like their kind of fun.

"Well, Dad said I have to earn it," Sarah explained. "He'll make me do lots of chores. I'll probably have to muck stalls and stack hay. It might not be worth it."

Willa nodded. She didn't care how much manure she had to shovel. She'd clean out a hundred stalls if she could ride a horse in that parade.

Chapter 2

THE NEXT AFTERNOON WILLA, SARAH, AND
Sarah's little sister, Bess, were sitting in the
deep grass right next to the Starlings' pasture.

Sarah was listing all the things she had to
do before she could ride in the parade. "And
I also have to babysit Bess more," she complained.

As cute as Bess was, Willa knew she could

be a handful. "She's kind of quiet today," Willa commented.

"Yeah. Ever since we got Buttercup, all she wants to do is feed her," Sarah replied.

"She likes how, every once in a while, Buttercup just takes off. She'll gallop across the field and throw in a couple of bucks here and there. Bess cracks up every time. She loves it."

"Pretty horsey," Bess whispered as she picked clover stems and made a bouquet. "Pretty Buttercup."

Buttercup was a tall, slender horse with a glistening chestnut coat. She had a small star between her warm eyes. But every once in a while, those eyes sparkled with real mischief.

Willa wondered how the horse got her name. She looked nothing like the small yellow flower that grew like a weed in the summertime.

"Does she like to eat buttercups?" Willa thought out loud.

"I doubt it. They taste horrible," Sarah said. "See how they're all over the pasture? They're too bitter, so no one eats them. Not even the goats."

Willa laughed out loud. Even though they'd

known the other family only a month, she and Ben had already seen the Starlings' goats eat a gym shoe, a juice box, and one of Bess's dirty diapers. Actually, Mrs. Starling had rescued the diaper just in time, but not the shoe. When Chipper finally wrestled it from Kirby, just a shoelace was left.

"At least the horses keep her in one place," Willa said, nodding at Bess.

"No joke," Sarah agreed. "Dad calls her Houdini in pigtails." Willa wasn't surprised that they compared Bess to the famous magician. She was a real escape artist. "Chipper says we should get some kind of tracking device for her."

Just then Willa heard Ben's laughter. It was getting closer.

"Stop him!" Chipper called out. "He's out of control!" The boys were chasing a puppy.

Sarah jumped up. "Amos!" she cried.

Willa was on her feet in seconds too. All four kids raced after the black-and-white pup with the bright pink tongue. Amos zigged and zagged. The kids' fingers groped and grabbed, but no one could catch him. Finally he ran under the pasture fence and stopped, panting, next to Buttercup.

The horse turned her big head and snuffled at the puppy. Amos sniffed back, then licked the horse's muzzle.

"That's so cute!" Willa squealed.

"They always do that," Chipper insisted, resting his hands on his knees while he caught his breath.

"Always? *Really?* We just got Buttercup yesterday," Sarah pointed out.

"But I've seen Amos lick her like that, like, four times."

"Well, they'd better not get too attached," Sarah warned. "We have to start giving the puppies away soon."

Amos was one of seven puppies. The Starlings' dog, Marnie, had had puppies earlier that summer.

"Have you decided which one you're going to keep?" Ben asked.

"I like Amos," Chipper said. "He's fun, but Mom wants someone to adopt him."

"He'd be too much work," Sarah explained. "I really like Rice Cake and Jubilee. I think they'd be happy getting to stay with Marnie, but Dad says we can only keep one."

It seemed like everyone on Chincoteague had pets to spare, except Willa and Ben. Of course, they did have New Cat, but she wasn't really a pet. New Cat's job was to keep the mice away, and she was very good at it. Yes, she was soft and sweet, but she was a homebody. She didn't do tricks or go on adventures with Ben and Willa.

"Rice Cake and Jubilee might want to stay with their mom, but Amos looks like he's more attached to Buttercup," Ben observed. The puppy was playfully running loops around the tall mare. Buttercup did her best to ignore him. When he stopped and yipped, Buttercup snorted and trotted to the other side of the pasture. Amos followed her.

"He's trying to herd Buttercup," Chipper announced with a laugh.

"Buttercup!" Bess cried, holding out a giant bouquet of fresh clover. "Buttercup, come back! Buttercup!"

"Bess, leave her alone. Buttercup needs to get settled so I can ride Sweetums in the parade." Sarah stood up and grabbed her little sister by the hand, trying to tug her away. "Maybe we should take her down to the dock," Sarah suggested, looking at her brother.

"Ben and I have to get going," Willa said. "Our grandparents should be back by now."

"Do you have to go?" Sarah said. It now seemed funny to Willa that she and Sarah had not become friends as soon as they met. . . . At first, Willa thought Sarah was bossy and rude. That seemed so long ago!

"They're expecting us," Willa said, not wanting to hurt Sarah's feelings. Besides, it was the truth. At least, it was part of the truth. The whole truth was that Willa didn't want to spend the whole day fussing over Buttercup, Sweetums, and Bess. She wanted to see Starbuck, who was the most wonderful pony Willa had ever known.

"Yeah," Ben agreed. "They'll have stuff for us to do." Willa smiled at her brother. He was anxious to see Starbuck too.

♥

Starbuck greeted them with a happy whinny. "I think she hears the rattle of our bikes," Ben said as they propped the kickstands into place. "She just calls out. She doesn't even lift her head all the way to make sure it's us."

Grandma Edna looked up from her sweeping. "Animals have a sixth sense," she said. "For weather, for food, for danger. They rely on their instincts." She grabbed a long lead and headed for the paddock gate. "That mare's got good instincts. She's always been certain about you two."

Willa smiled. Grandma Edna was no-nonsense. She gave compliments only when she really meant them.

When Starbuck had first arrived, she'd been

hurt. The pony had limped because her leg was sore. Being a vet, Grandma Edna had known how to treat it. Willa and Ben had helped, wrapping the leg and keeping Starbuck company in the stall. But they'd never been allowed to ride her. Not yet.

"We've got to get this pony some exercise," Grandma said. "She has to be in shape if we're going to find her a new home."

Ben and Willa let out matching sighs. Neither could think about Starbuck going to another home—unless it was theirs.

"I'm going to play with Bee Bee Bun," Ben announced. Bee Bee Bun was an angora rabbit that was missing half an ear but had all his personality.

"That's good," Grandma said. "You can help

Clifton clean his hutch." Ben nodded. Clifton was a high school boy who helped around the barn. Clifton wanted to be a vet, and Ben thought that was super cool.

Willa and Grandma stood in the center of the paddock. Starbuck circled them on the long lead. "Give her a click. Get her to trot," Grandma directed.

Willa clicked her tongue, and the pony sped up. "Well, look at that," Grandma murmured. "She can move." The pony had a long, even stride.

Willa thought Starbuck looked beautiful. She wondered what it would be like to ride the pony. "Sarah might get to ride in the carnival parade," Willa said, surprising herself. She hadn't planned on telling Grandma.

"Is that so?" Grandma replied.

"The Starlings got a new horse," Willa explained. "So Sarah would ride Sweetums."

"Sweetums is a mighty fine horse," Grandma said. "But that parade is a mess. I wouldn't trust most horses with such a young rider. Someone's likely to get hurt."

Willa felt a knot in her belly. Was Grandma right?

"Hi, Mrs. Miller!" a voice rang out. Willa found its owner right away—a girl with long braids pulled into a low, thick ponytail. Her smile stretched all the way across her face.

"My parents sent me for Clifton." Before Grandma could respond, the girl spoke again. "You must be Willa! I'm Lena. I'm so excited to finally meet you! Sarah told me all about you in her letters. I've been away at piano camp, but now I'm back and we'll hang out. You, me, and Sarah will be like the three musketeers!"

"Okay," Willa said softly.

"Hey, sis." Clifton came up behind her and tugged on one of her many braids. "I heard you a mile away. We should go."

With that, Clifton picked up Lena, plopped her on his bike seat, and put a helmet on her head.

"Willa! Come to the ice-cream parlor at three tomorrow," Lena instructed. "It's my birthday."

Grandma chuckled to herself. "That girl's got ten words for every one from her brother."

Willa watched as they rode away. Willa's friendship with Sarah had been very slow to start, but Lena was great gangbusters.

Chapter 3

THE NEXT DAY, SARAH PICKED UP WILLA FOR the party. Chipper and Ben were going too. "Lena's lots of fun," Sarah said, "except she doesn't like horses."

"That's weird," Willa said before she could stop herself. They were walking to Lena's party at Four Corners, taking a shortcut on a side street.

"She doesn't hate them or anything," Sarah replied. "But her parents won't let her ride. They're worried she'll fall off and get hurt. Then she couldn't play piano."

"Not if she broke her leg," Chipper said. "She could still play then."

"You should tell her parents," Sarah said. "Maybe they'll change their minds." Chipper and Ben both rolled their eyes. Big sisters.

Grandma Edna had mentioned that Lena was a good musician. Sarah had said that Lena was not allowed to play until she had practiced piano for an hour each day. Willa had known kids like that back in Chicago.

It felt funny, going to the birthday party of someone she barely knew. Luckily, Willa and Ben were going in on Sarah and Chipper's gift for Lena. "It's a huge boxed set of mystery books," Sarah had explained. "Lena loves detective stories and spooky stuff."

Willa would never have guessed that! She would have had no clue if she had had to choose a gift for Lena.

"Hey! Hey!"

Willa spotted Lena in the middle of the outside courtyard, surrounded by bunches of silver balloons. Clifton was there, along with some other kids Willa and Sarah's age.

"Check it out," Lena said, rushing up to the fence. She pointed to a turquoise bike. It wasn't an ordinary bike. It was raised up on a stand so it wouldn't go anywhere. Plus, it had extra gears that were attached to a wooden bucket. "We're going to ride this bike and

make the energy to churn the ice cream."

Willa had never seen anything like it. "We can really make that much energy? On a bike?"

Lena nodded. "Whatever we make I get to take home."

"I'm next!" yelled Chipper. He rushed forward and climbed through the fence's wooden rails.

"Then me!" Ben said, right on Chipper's heels. They lined up next to the bike.

Willa bit her lip. At least Ben wasn't worried about fitting in.

Sarah grabbed her hand. Willa ducked under the fence behind her friend. Sarah was great. She introduced her to all the other kids. Then Lena motioned for them to sit down with her at the center picnic table.

"This is a big party," Willa said.

"I know," Lena admitted. "My mom's on the PTA and she works at the museum, so I have to invite *everyone*." She pushed her beaded braids over her shoulder. "But even if it were a small party, I would have invited you, Willa."

Willa smiled, but she didn't know what to say to the birthday girl.

"Hey, Sarah," a kid called from the line by the bike. "Bet I can make more energy than you." Sarah glanced over her shoulder but then turned back around. "Time me," he yelled. "I can go five minutes."

"I don't think so," Sarah answered, not even making eye contact with the boy. As soon as he had taken his place on the bike, Sarah glared at Lena. "Yick," she whispered. "Did you have to invite Jasper Langely?" Willa had never seen

Sarah look so disgusted, not even when Sarah stepped in their barn cat's throw-up—in her bare feet.

Lena leaned forward as if the three girls were sharing the juiciest secret. "Jasper's not that bad. My mom always works with his mom at the carnival." Willa glanced at the boy again. In the midday sun, she could see sweat popping up where his pale blond hair parted. He scowled as his legs whizzed around on the pedals.

Sarah turned to Willa. "He has been in my class every year. He's pretty smart, but he always wants to bet on who will get the best grade on a test. It's annoying."

"You should take that bet," Lena suggested. "You always get the highest score."

"Nope," Sarah said, smoothing the creases

from her skirt. "If I say yes once, he'll bug me all the time. He will bet on anything!"

A few minutes later Jasper called to Sarah again. "I bet I've churned enough ice cream for three giant sundaes."

"Good!" Lena responded. "That's enough for Sarah, Willa, and me. Thanks."

"Come on, Sarah," Jasper begged. "Take a turn."

"No," Sarah replied. "I'm saving my energy for barn chores so I can ride in the carnival parade."

"No way!" Jasper exclaimed, climbing off the bike. "How come you get to ride? You haven't before."

"Neither have you." Sarah turned to face Jasper. After a pause, she added, "My dad got a new horse, so he's going to let me ride Sweetums."

"That old nag? I'm riding my dad's horse, Wrangler."

"Sweetums isn't old," Willa said, defending Sarah's favorite.

"Like you know anything about horses," Jasper said, looking Willa up and down. "You aren't even from Chincoteague."

Willa felt a knot in her stomach. How could he say that?

Jasper turned back to Sarah. "There's no way you'll get to ride."

"Oh, yeah?" Sarah questioned.

"Yeah. You wanna bet?"

"Sure."

It wasn't long before they agreed on the

terms of the bet. All Sarah had to do was ride in the parade, and she would win. If she didn't get to ride, she would lose. The loser had to buy the winner the biggest ice-cream sundae on the Four Corners menu.

"It's a deal." Jasper and Sarah shook hands.

"Whoa, the biggest sundae? That's the one with the homemade brownie, the caramel, and the fudge," Lena pointed out.

"I know," Sarah said. "It's my favorite. I *have* to win. And prove that Jasper Langely doesn't know everything!"

Chapter 4

THE DAY AFTER THE PARTY, WILLA HAD an idea. It was a great idea. If Sarah was doing chores to be in the parade, maybe she could too. More than anything, Willa would love to ride Starbuck in the parade. But that was a long shot. She hadn't even been able to ride Starbuck at Miller Farm yet. Still, Willa was willing to do lots of chores. She wanted

Grandma to see how responsible she could be.

"I need to go to Miller Farm," Willa announced at breakfast. "I'm going to ask Grandma Edna if I can have some regular chores."

"That's a great idea," Mom said between sips of coffee. "Why don't you start here first? I'll give you chores."

Willa's shoulders drooped. "What kind of chores?"

"Any kind. All kinds!" Mom sounded excited. "When the inn opens up, this place is going to have to run like clockwork. Your dad and I will need your help."

Hearing this, Willa had a hard time swallowing her toast. Ben had a hard time hiding a smirk, until Mom spoke again. "Ben, you'll need some chores of your own." His smirk disappeared.

After breakfast, the brother and sister met in Willa's room. Willa had a clipboard. "We have to make a list of chores. Chores we can do, so the house runs like clockwork," Willa said.

"Our house will never run like clockwork. Unless the clock is broken," Ben said.

It was a joke, but it was also true. The Dunlaps had bad habits. They ran late. Their dirty laundry piles grew to the size of mountains. Mail and homework stacks were lopsided towers on the dinner table.

"Why did you have to volunteer us for chores?" Ben asked.

"I wanted to do chores at the farm, so I can ride in the parade," Willa explained. "Like Sarah."

"You think Mom would let you?" Ben asked.

"Yeah. But Grandma is going to be a harder sell." Willa had heard her dad use that phrase. It meant that it wasn't easy to convince someone. It would be hard to sell them on your idea. Grandma Edna might be the hardest sell of all time.

"Yeah, you're right. But riding in the parade would be fun," admitted Ben. "We'd be real Chincoteague kids then."

Willa looked at Ben. He had a faraway look in his eyes. Did he want to ride in the parade too?

"Let's start in the bathroom," Willa said. "First off, towels should not be on the floor. We have a towel rack for that."

Ben rolled his eyes. "The towels always slip off," he complained.

"Then use the hook on the back of the door,"

Willa suggested as she filled out her chore chart. "Let's look at your room."

They came up with a good list together.

Throw dirty clothes in the laundry basket.

Make beds.

Park bikes in the barn.

Sweep decks.

Water flowers.

"I also told Mom we'd put our dirty dishes in the sink and take turns setting the table," Willa said after they had taken a full tour of the house.

"I told her we'd feed New Cat," Ben told his sister.

"That seems like a good start," Willa stated, hoping they'd still have time for chores at Miller Farm.

"I also said we'd look after Mrs. Cornett's chickens," Ben added, "but only when they get in our yard." Their neighbor had a lot of chickens. Some of the chickens liked to visit the Dunlaps' backyard. The hens pecked in the grass and at the orange flowers on the fence. Ben really liked the chickens.

"Okay," murmured Willa. "Let's not volunteer for anything else, or we won't have any time left."

"Okay," agreed Ben. The two went to find Mom.

"This will be so helpful," Mom said as she reviewed the checklist. "You can get started now. Once you're done, you can go to Sarah and Chipper's or the farm. Grandma said she wants you there first thing tomorrow. She said it's going to be a big day."

Willa's mind leaped at the news. A big day? They were going to get to ride Starbuck. She was sure of it! She really wanted to tell Sarah, but she didn't want to jinx it. She closed her eyes and wished she were right.

♥

"Buttercup is acting weird," Sarah said when Willa arrived at the Starlings'. "She's not as peppy as when she showed up."

"Maybe she was just showing off at first," Chipper said. "Maybe she's not a peppy pony at all."

Sarah shook her head.

"Buttercup," Bess yodeled, waving a fistful of grass and clover. "Flowers for Buttercup!" Bess thrust them through the fence.

The tall chestnut horse dragged her hooves

over to Bess. She reached out her long, neck and nibbled at the stems in Bess's hand.

"Dad just looked at her this morning and sighed," Sarah said. "What if he decides not to ride Buttercup in the parade?"

Willa knew exactly what Sarah was thinking. Of course she was concerned about the new horse, but it was more than that. If Mr. Starling didn't ride Buttercup in the parade, Sarah couldn't ride Sweetums. If Sarah didn't ride Sweetums, Sarah would lose the bet with Jasper.

Chapter 5

THE NEXT MORNING, WILLA AND BEN RODE THEIR
bikes to their grandparents' place in near silence.
They were both thinking of the same thing.

"You can go first," Willa said. They propped
their bikes against the far side of the farmhouse
and then hurried to the barn.

"How come you're letting me go?" Ben
asked.

"Can't I do something nice?" responded Willa. She tried to sound offended, but Ben had a right to be suspicious. Willa did want to get on Starbuck as soon as she could. However, she also had a plan. She suspected she would get a longer turn if she went second.

"Doesn't she look lovely?" Grandma Edna asked. She had already tacked up Starbuck. A fluffy white pad rested under the saddle on her back. The leather bridle brought out the deep chocolate brown of her eyes and mane. "I can tell by the look on your faces that your mom already told you."

"She just said it was a big day," replied Willa.

"Well, it is," Grandma declared. "You'll be riding Starbuck."

The three of them headed out to the small paddock together. There, the grassy ground was softer. It would be easier on Starbuck's newly healed leg.

The normally calm pony's ears twitched in every direction, and she gave a quick snort. "She's ready," Grandma Edna said, pushing a helmet into Ben's hands. "Are you?"

"I think so," Ben mumbled.

"You can't be wishy-washy with horses, Ben," Grandma Edna insisted. "Horses need a sure hand." Ben knew that tone; it was just like Willa's. He tried to remember if Grandma Edna was also a big sister.

"I know," Ben declared. "I am ready." He may not have had all the riding lessons Willa had back in Chicago, but he loved Starbuck every bit as much. He put his left foot in the stirrup and pulled himself up.

"There you go," Grandma said. She gave Starbuck a slap on the rump, and the pony moved to the far end of the lead line. Grandma stood in the middle, and Starbuck walked around her.

"How about a trot?" Grandma Edna clicked her tongue, and Starbuck picked up her pace.

It was fun. Ben couldn't believe he was riding Starbuck. He and Willa had waited so long! He had gone around the small circle several times before he started feeling woozy.

"Grandma, I think he's getting dizzy," Willa warned.

"No, I'm not," Ben protested, but his head churned like a blender. He felt like he might slide right out of the saddle.

"He looks good," said Grandma, full of pride.

Ben felt his body start to tilt.

"Whoa, that's enough, Ben." Grandma Edna stopped the merry-go-round just in time. Ben still felt woozy on the ground. He heard Willa giggle as he stumbled off toward the barn.

"Nice and easy," Grandma called out to Willa, who was rushing toward Starbuck. Dust rose up from under her boots. Her excitement was bubbling and bursting in every muscle. She had to force herself to slow down to a walk.

"You need to be steady, Willa. You never want to startle a horse. They'll suspect danger."

Willa knew this. She knew that in the wild horses had to be alert. They were always on the lookout. But it was hard to be "nice and easy" when she was so close!

She took a deep breath as she grabbed the saddle. She hoisted herself up. Her toes searched for the stirrups, and she pushed her weight into her heels.

Willa could hardly believe it. She ran her hand along the pony's neck. Starbuck was soft and warm and wonderful.

"Ask her to walk on," Grandma instructed.

As soon as Willa squeezed her legs around Starbuck's belly, the pony responded.

"And trot."

Willa clicked her tongue, and Starbuck sprang ahead.

Willa's rear popped out of the saddle with each bouncy step. Even though the lead line was attached to the pony's bridle, it was still fun. Starbuck had a happy stride.

In no time, Grandma had them turn around. "Want to try it without the lead, steering on your own?" she asked.

"Yes!"

Grandma started to pull them in.

"Edna, phone!" Grandpa's yell came from the house.

"Just a minute!" Grandma called back as she unclipped the lead from the bridle. "Hold tight," she said, giving Starbuck a pat. "I'll be right back."

Starbuck stamped her foot, so Willa let the pony walk in the paddock. It was going so well, Willa wondered if they might get to try to canter. Willa liked to canter most of all. What if Starbuck could jump? How soon would they get to try that?

The door slammed. Grandma marched out, arms swinging at her sides.

"That'll be it for today," she said.

"But—" Willa started to say when Grandma clutched at the bridle, and Starbuck stopped.

"Sorry to cut it short, sweetie." Grandma's voice had turned soft, but her words were still hurried. "The Starlings' new horse is sick, real sick, and you have to come with me."

Willa's heart fell to her foot as she lowered herself to the dusty ground. Sure, she was disappointed at not being able to keep riding, but her thoughts had now leaped to Sarah . . . and to Buttercup.

Chapter 6

WHEN GRANDMA EDNA, WILLA, AND BEN arrived, everyone at the Starlings' place was quiet. Even Lena, who had come over to try to cheer up Sarah, did not smile.

"What seems to be the problem?" Grandma Edna asked, still a dozen steps away from the pasture gate.

Mr. Starling unlatched the lock to open it for

her. "Buttercup's been lazy for the past couple of days," he explained. "It was quite a change. She was a real spark plug when she first got here."

Willa remembered the horse playing with Amos, the mischievous puppy. Whenever Amos nipped at her leg, she had run away across the field. She had seemed very lively—and hungry for clover and grass.

Now Buttercup looked weary. Her head drooped. She hardly twitched an ear when Grandma approached. Mr. Starling held Buttercup's halter and talked softly while Grandma took a good, long look.

She sighed and ran her hands over the horse's legs. After rummaging in her kit, she pulled out a stethoscope and pressed it to the horse's belly. Next, she moved to Buttercup's head.

"There's something not right," Grandma agreed. "Her eyes are dull. Her lips are swollen. Tender gums." Wearing thin gloves, Grandma felt all around Buttercup's mouth. "What's she been eating?"

Mr. Starling went on to explain that Buttercup had been eating all the same things as Sweetums: same hay, same grain, same grass. "They got along so well, they've been in the same field from the start. I don't get why Buttercup is sick but Sweetums is fine. I don't think it's the food."

Grandma made her way to the center of the pasture and kneeled down. Willa wondered, *What is she doing?* She had a twig and was poking in a pile of something. *Yuck! Horse manure!*

"Things look okay here," Grandma said. "Not too hard or too runny. You should watch for any changes. And I'd like to check your bag of grain, just in case," Grandma said. "There's also the chance that Buttercup got hold of something poisonous. I'm sure you know that buttercups are toxic." Grandma pointed to the tall, straggly plants in the pasture, each with clusters of tiny yellow flowers at the top.

Mr. Starling nodded. "Horses don't touch it. It's too bitter."

Grandma walked over to the nearest buttercup plant and tugged. The tough stem came out roots and all. "Let's just make sure," she said as she walked back and offered Buttercup the

delicate flowers. Buttercup gave a lazy sniff and turned away.

"I'll think on it, Lloyd. The horse is not herself, but she's not too bad off." She watched Buttercup as she loaded up her vet kit. "We'd best keep an eye on her. I can run some tests if she doesn't improve." The two adults headed to the barn to look at the grain. Bess was behind them, picking clover as she went.

"Where are the puppies?" Ben asked. Willa

rolled her eyes. Didn't he care about Buttercup at all?

"They're with Marnie," Chipper said. "Amos won't leave Buttercup alone, so Dad made us put them all in the outdoor pen, at least until the vet is gone. Your grandma, I mean."

"Let's go get them," Ben said, taking off.

The girls didn't want to leave Buttercup.

As soon as the boys were gone, Sarah blurted out, "I feel so bad. I keep thinking about the parade instead of worrying about Buttercup."

"My daddy always tells me worrying won't do you any good," Lena said. "You've got to do something."

"What can we do?" Willa asked.

"I don't know." Lena paused. "But I do know is

that it's a mystery," she said, her words drawn out to sound spooky. "No, seriously. We should get to the bottom of it. First off, who are our suspects?"

Sarah and Willa glanced at each other.

"This isn't one of your mystery books, Lena. There *aren't* any suspects," Sarah protested. "Buttercup is probably just sick."

"But we don't know for sure," Lena insisted.

"Jasper!" Willa had no idea why she had yelled that name. Sarah glared at her.

"What?" Willa tried to defend herself. "He doesn't want to lose the bet."

"Sarah, you are the one who said how much he likes to win bets," Lena reminded her friend. "That is a motive."

Sarah's shoulders rose as she took a deep breath. "I guess so."

"Great," Lena said. "That's one."

Willa didn't think it was great at all. A horse was sick, and they were accusing someone of poisoning that horse. It seemed horrible!

"We need more suspects." Lena narrowed her eyes, thinking. "What about your dad, Sarah?"

"Lena!" Sarah yelled. "Stop it. This isn't a game. My dad would never do that." She stared at the ground.

"Are you okay?" Willa asked.

"I'm fine, but can we please talk about something else?" She pushed her thick hair behind her ear. She refused to look at Lena.

"Whatever you want," Lena replied with a shrug. "But you won't solve a case by ignoring it."

Willa stared at Lena. She was using all these real detective words. Did she think she was a *real* detective?

Lena started to leave. When she was halfway across the yard, she turned around and walked backward. She pointed at Sarah with both hands. "You know what you need?" she asked excitedly. "A *stakeout*. That way, you'll know if someone is coming by and poisoning Buttercup. And you'll catch him red-handed!"

Willa's eyes grew wide. She couldn't believe Lena! She shook her head and turned to Sarah as Lena walked away.

Sarah tilted her head to one side. Then she titled it to the other. Finally she said to Willa, "A stakeout is not a bad idea. We should do it. Tonight."

Chapter 7

SARAH INSISTED THAT THEY HAVE THE STAKE-out that night. The Summer Extravaganza was only a week away, so there wasn't a lot of time. Even though the stakeout had been Lena's idea, Sarah and Willa were not sure they should invite her.

"She's not always like that," Sarah said. "Maybe it's because we gave her all those books."

"Maybe."

"She's probably been reading those mysteries nonstop since the party," said Sarah. "And this isn't the first time she's done this. She's insisted that something was a *real* mystery before."

After she had given it some thought, Willa decided Lena should join them. It was kind of cool, the way Lena could think like a detective. Willa just didn't want her to upset Sarah.

"We can make it fun. With a tent, sleeping bags, and flashlights," Sarah said. "Mom will make us invite the boys, but we won't tell them it's a stakeout."

Willa agreed that was a good idea. Otherwise, Ben would bring his binoculars, his walkie-talkie with all the beeping buttons, and the long-range water shooter he got for his birthday. They would never get any detective work done! The more she thought about it, the more excited Willa was for that night.

"We can set up the tent here," Sarah said, standing with her arms stretched out. "It's close to the field but not too close. I'll get the tent. Will you ask my mom if you can call Lena?"

Willa went into the house in search of Mrs. Starling. She found her at the kitchen table with a computer and several dictionaries. Mrs. Starling was a book translator.

When Willa called and talked to Lena, she did not mention the stakeout. "Just tell her it's a sleepover," Sarah had said.

But Lena knew the truth at once. "A stakeout is the right thing to do," she said. "I'll bring the marshmallows."

"Great," was Willa's only reply.

Mrs. Starling smiled when Willa handed back the phone. She paused her typing for a moment and adjusted her blue-rimmed glasses. "I used to love outdoor sleepovers," she said. "I wish I weren't so busy, I'd sleep out with you."

"Maybe next time," Willa suggested. Willa really liked Mrs. Starling. With all the kids and animals, the Starlings' house always seemed so fun and lively.

"I'd like that. I hope Bess isn't giving you too much trouble out there." Mrs. Starling mentioned her youngest daughter as she went back to her typing. "You kids are such a help with her."

Willa gave a quick, nervous smile and rushed outside. Where *was* little Bess? She had to find Sarah. "Sarah!" she called. "Sarah?" she repeated when her friend didn't answer.

Sarah came out of the garage. "What?"

"Do you know where Bess is?" Willa asked.

Sarah's eyes immediately filled with worry. "She must be with the boys. They're out back."

They raced to the other side of the house to find Ben and Chipper playing fetch with the puppies. Ben was flat on the ground, being licked by three puppies at once.

"Where's Bess?"

Chipper's face was blank. "I thought she was with *you*."

Willa's heart began to pound.

"No, she's not," Sarah said. "And she's not

with Mom." She looked around the yard. "You guys go down to the dock. Willa will check the fields. I'll look along the street. Now go!"

Everyone ran off. Willa's mind raced in time with her legs. She hadn't even thought about the dock. The very back of the Starlings' yard went down to the bay. It was the stretch of water between Chincoteague and Assateague. She hoped little Bess would not have gone to the water alone.

Willa forced her mind back to the pasture and the fields. If she didn't find Bess there, she'd go to the barn. Her breath was short when she stopped by the pasture fence. She grabbed hold of one of the wooden posts and climbed up for a better view. The pasture had

a trough,

two horses,

one puppy named Amos,

and a lot of grass and bitter yellow flowers.

No Bess.

"Bess!" Willa called. She turned to the field. At first she didn't see anything. Then she noticed something stirring in the waist-high grass. "Bess!" she cried, and ran. Bess was sitting deep in a patch of red clover.

"Sarah! Sarah! I found her!"

After a moment Bess held up a bundle of flowers. "For Buttercup," she announced. "A snack."

Willa smiled and nodded. "Horses love that sweet clover, don't they?" she said, kneeling down. She didn't hear Sarah approach.

"Willa? Bess? Where are you guys?" Sarah pleaded. Willa stood up and waved.

At once Sarah plunged into the tall grass, grabbed Bess under the arms, and lifted the small girl to her hip. "We were so worried," she said.

"She was picking a snack for Buttercup," Willa explained.

"Bess, you can't do that. You can't run off. And you can't feed Buttercup. The vet said no extra food until Buttercup gets better." Sarah brushed the pollen off her sister's pink cheek and squeezed her small body close.

It already felt like a long day, so Willa was sure her parents would say no to the sleepover. Willa and Ben had not been home much in the past week, other than to do their chores. They had spent a lot of time with the Starlings and with Starbuck.

"A sleepover? That sounds great!" Mom

exclaimed. "Are you sure the Starlings don't mind?"

"Not at all," Willa answered, stealing a pinch of shredded cheese from the counter. "Mr. Starling already put up the tent."

"Well, that works out perfectly. It'll give us a chance to clean up," Mom said. She hurried down the hallway and opened the closet. It was full of all kinds of tools and supplies. "The carpenters finished their work on the fence and deck today. I want to paint, and it's better if you and your sticky fingers aren't around."

Willa grinned. For once, being messy paid off.

Chapter 8

"YOUR DAD MAKES GOOD CHILI, WILLA," LENA said. It was later that evening. The sleepover had begun, but the sleeping had not. Lena leaned back into one of the beanbag chairs the girls had dragged out from Sarah's house just before the sun set.

The girls were each eating a cup of Willa's dad's soup, and Ben and Chipper were off in the dark, searching for fireflies.

"Thanks. He'd be happy to hear you say that," Willa said, blowing on the lumpy red beans on her spoon. "My family is sick of testing

chili. We've tried, like, a dozen recipes over the past two weeks. After we eat, my dad always quizzes us. He expects us to know if he's put in one tablespoon of cumin or two. He really wants to win the chili cook-off at the carnival, but he's driving us crazy!"

"That *is* crazy," Lena agreed, waving her spoon in the air. "My dad always makes the exact same recipe every time."

"And he always wins the Greater Chincoteague Chili Cook-Off," Sarah added. "*Every* time."

Willa's eyebrows shot up.

"Yeah," Lena admitted. "But I really like your dad's. It tastes like there's extra oregano."

Willa's eyebrows shot up even further. Her dad had said something about oregano when she'd tasted the chili earlier that day. Could

Lena really taste that? Maybe she did have superdetective skills after all!

"My mom keeps warning my dad that he shouldn't do anything too fancy," Willa said. "She said that people on the island like their traditions."

"They do!" Sarah agreed. "And there's something special about always having Mr. Wise's chili at the Summer Extravaganza. It just tastes right."

"Well, my dad includes a special ingredient," Lena admitted. "It's a secret."

A secret ingredient? Willa frowned. Her dad had his work cut out for him.

"So," Lena whispered, moving in closer, "the boys don't know this is a stakeout?"

"It's just a sleepover," Sarah insisted.

"Yeah, right," Lena said. "And the Triple Fudge Caramel Brownie Surprise is just another bowl of ice cream." Lena paused to take a bite of corn bread. "You are worried about Buttercup, *and* you want to win that bet. Those are two good reasons for a stakeout." She took another bite. "Don't worry. I will be discreet, and I can stay up late."

Willa smirked. Her friends back in Chicago never used words like *discreet*. It *was* the perfect word to say that she could keep a secret and wouldn't make a big deal about it. Lena knew how to say what she meant. Willa admired that.

Sarah sighed. "All right. We should keep an eye out. I want to find out what's going on, but I hope I can keep my eyes open."

♥

The three girls were quiet for a while. They could hear the boys running after the fire-flies, whooping every time they caught or missed one.

"If they aren't quiet, they'll scare away all the suspects," Lena mumbled.

Willa didn't want to believe there were any *real* suspects. Why would anyone want to poison Buttercup?

They ate super-gooey s'mores with peanut-butter cups melted inside. They counted bats swooping through the sky. They wondered who their teacher would be in the fall.

But they didn't see anything suspicious.

When it was time for bed, the boys joined them. They could all fit in the Starlings' enormous tent—the sleeping bags didn't even touch! Lena held a flashlight to her chin and told a spooky story about a ghost horse, the shadows playing across her face. Even though there was a sick horse in the pasture nearby, no one seemed to mind. The story was *that* good.

Willa couldn't guess how late it was when Mr. Starling made them turn off their flash-lights. There were annoying mosquitoes, but Lena insisted they sleep with the tent flaps open. "How else will we see anything?" she asked when Sarah protested.

Early the next morning Willa woke with a ⌐ in her face. Actually, she woke up just *after* a foot had been in her face. "Yuck! Ow! Ben?"

"Sorry," he said as he tripped out of the tent. Chipper followed him.

Willa poked Sarah and then Lena. "Did you see anyone? Did you hear anything? Did you see our suspect?" Willa asked. She propped herself up on her elbows.

"Not a thing. No one came by at all." Lena rubbed her eyes with her fingertips. She sat cross-legged with her pillow in her lap.

"At least no one that we saw," Sarah corrected.

"I told you, I can stay up late," Lena said. "I'm pretty sure no one came by. I would have seen him . . . or her."

Willa took a closer look at Lena. Her eyes looked red! "You look like you didn't sleep at all."

Lena raised her eyebrows. "That's a good observation."

Had Lena stayed up all night? The detective stood up and started to shove her sleeping bag into its tiny duffel. "I've got to go home."

"But Mom will make pancakes," said Sarah. "Maybe with whipped cream."

"No, thanks," Lena answered. "I don't want pancakes. I just want my own bed."

At the breakfast table Mr. Starling told the girls he had checked on Buttercup that morning, and she was about the same. He shook his head. "She's got the same puffy lips. The same dull eyes."

"The same stinky manure," Chipper added.

"Chipper, we're eating!" scolded Sarah.

"What?" he asked. "Ben's grandma told us to keep an eye on it. We have to make sure it doesn't get too runny."

"It's good that you're helpful, dear," Mrs. Starling said.

Ben nudged Chipper with his elbow, and both boys snorted.

Sarah pulled Willa aside after breakfast. "You know," she began, "there must be some way we can find out if Jasper is behind Buttercup being sick."

"I agree," Willa said, leaning against the family-room wall. "But just so you know, I don't think it's him. I only yelled out his name because Lena was being so pushy."

"Don't worry. She gets like that," Sarah answered.

"Well, what should we do?"

Sarah looked Willa in the eye. "We can ask him."

Why hadn't Willa thought of that?

Chapter 9

WILLA AND SARAH HOPPED ON THEIR BIKES
and headed to the other side of the island. They
hoped Jasper would be around to answer their
questions.

Sarah knocked on the door. Jasper's mom
smiled when she saw her. Sarah introduced
Willa and said they had a question for Jasper.
His mom said he was in the backyard.

"That seemed easy," Willa whispered.

They rounded the corner and immediately saw Jasper—sitting in a kiddie pool, reading comics.

"What are *you* doing here?" he asked, quickly standing up. A trickle of water ran off his swimming trunks. "Trying to get out of our bet?" He sounded pretty sure of himself.

"Maybe you wanted to get a look at Wrangler. He's in the barn."

"Not really," Sarah said. "I actually have a question for you. It's kind of weird." Sarah went on to explain how sick Buttercup was. It took a while, but Jasper's jaw dropped when he realized what Sarah was hinting at.

"That's horrible!" he exclaimed. "I would never do that to a horse. I mean, it's just a bet. It's just a bowl of ice cream."

A picture of the extra-large scoops topped with a brownie and caramel flashed in Willa's head. It wasn't just *any* bowl of ice cream, but she totally believed Jasper. By the look on his face, he would never do anything to hurt a horse.

"That's what I thought," Sarah said, shoving

her hands in her pockets. "We just had to make sure. We're following all our leads."

Willa almost laughed, but Jasper looked serious. "I'm sorry your horse is sick. I'll let you know if I think of anything." He pressed his lips together. "I'll let you out of the bet if you want."

"No." Sarah shook her head. "A bet's a bet."

They said good-bye and headed back to their bikes. "'We're following all our leads'?" Willa said to her friend. "That's real detective talk. I'll have to tell Lena."

Sarah squealed. "Don't you dare!"

Willa laughed. It was a relief that Jasper was no longer a suspect, but they still didn't know what was wrong with Buttercup. And the carnival was less than a week away.

♥

Willa checked in with Sarah every day. Her friend had given up hope of being part of the parade. Buttercup was the same—no better, no worse. All week, both Willa and Ben helped out as much as they could, at home and at Miller Farm. They both had a chance to ride Starbuck again, with Grandma watching as closely as always. Their favorite pony was definitely healthy again.

One afternoon Grandma Edna offered them a ride on the beach as a special thank-you for all their help. Ben sat on Jake, the big draft horse. Grandma even let him take the reins. "Don't you worry," she said, patting Ben on the leg. "Jake likes to stay close to the others. He won't wander off." Ben sat tall in the saddle. He was twice his normal height!

Willa was just as pleased when Grandma

gave her permission to ride Starbuck. "Really?" she said.

"Well, why wouldn't I let you ride her? You two get along so well." Grandma Edna smoothed her hand along Starbuck's toffee-colored neck. "You're just about the steadiest mare ever, aren't you? I wouldn't trust just any pony with my granddaughter."

Willa wondered if she should tell Grandma that she wanted to ride in the parade, that she wanted to ride in the parade on Starbuck! But Willa decided not to say anything. For now, getting to ride Starbuck on the beach was more than enough.

Willa's mood was still happy as they rode home on their bikes. "Was it fun on Jake?" she yelled to Ben over her shoulder.

"It was awesome!" Ben declared. "I could see for miles!"

Horseback riding on the beach was always amazing. Willa loved to gaze over at Assateague and think about the wild ponies. It was hard to believe that Starbuck had been born on that tiny island—that she was once part of the sandy shore, the marsh grass, and the sea breeze.

As they approached the Starlings' place, Willa was trying to imagine Starbuck as a foal.

"Hey, look!" Ben called. "There's Bess. She's feeding Buttercup *again*."

Willa blinked and tried to focus. Sure enough, the little girl was right back at the pasture fence. She must have escaped from Sarah's supervision again.

"We have to tell the Starlings," Willa said,

swerving her bike into the gravel driveway.
Ben skidded to a stop behind her.

She pushed the doorbell three times, fast.
Then she ran toward the pasture.

Ben was just a few steps behind her. Mr.
Starling spotted him when he answered the
door. "Ben Dunlap, are you playing a trick on
me?" he called out. Sarah and Chipper's dad
had a jolly tone, until he saw Ben's face.

"It's Bess," Ben yelled. "She's by the pasture, sir."

Willa was already kneeling down next to
Bess, making sure she was okay. The little
girl had been leaning over the bottom board
of the fence, trying to get closer to her favorite horse.

"For Buttercup," Bess said, holding out another bouquet.

"Yes," Willa replied. "You picked clover for Buttercup."

Bess shook her head. *"Buttercups* for Buttercup," she declared.

Willa slowly took in the words. "Can I see?" she asked Bess hopefully.

Bess nodded and handed over the bouquet with pride.

Mr. Starling had arrived, with Ben and Sarah and Chipper close behind.

Willa stood up and held out the bouquet. "I think we might have solved the mystery," she said.

♥

It was hard to believe that Bess had been feeding Buttercup some of the toxic flowers. Willa called Grandma Edna from the Starlings' house to get advice.

"There was just one strand in the whole big bouquet," Willa explained. "When we asked Bess, she said that Buttercup didn't like the buttercup flowers, so she hid them in the clover. Bess wanted Buttercup to eat the buttercups because they had the same name."

Grandma said it was good news that the horse didn't like the taste of the flowers. "Since she wasn't that sick, I'm sure she'll recover. She didn't show any of the serious signs of poisoning. But you have to get the horse away from Bess. We can't have the little girl feeding the horse any more toxic plants."

Grandma had come up with an easy solution: Buttercup should live at Misty Inn for the time being. The workers had fixed the fence. Willa and Ben's mom had painted it. And there was a clean stall in the barn. Grandma called to make sure it was okay, and she promised to come by later to check on the horse. Willa was relieved that they'd solved the problem, but she doubted it was time to help Sarah win the bet. The parade was in just three days.

"We're going to have a horse living in our field? In our barn?" Ben could hardly believe it.

"It's awfully nice of your folks to take Buttercup in," Mr. Starling said as he led the mare out of the pasture.

"Bye-bye, Buttercup," Bess said from her

mother's arms. She sniffed and leaned her head on her mom's shoulder.

"It's okay," Willa said in her kindest voice. "She's not going very far. You can come visit her at our house."

Buttercup swished her tail and took her time on the short journey. Meanwhile, Amos yipped and ran circles around the whole traveling band.

"That puppy seems to have adopted Buttercup," noted Mr. Starling.

"Yeah," Ben said. "He's always sneaking into the pasture to see her. They're friends."

"It's not as odd as you might think," Mr. Starling said. "I'm afraid you might be getting more than one new animal as guests at your inn."

Willa locked eyes with Ben. Was Mr. Starling

saying what she thought he was saying? Willa crossed her fingers. It was great, knowing that they could offer Buttercup a safe, happy home, but if getting Amos was part of the deal, that would be even better.

Chapter 10

GRANDMA EDNA HAD BEEN RIGHT. THE SOLU-
tion was easy. Buttercup started to improve as
soon as she was at Misty Inn. The very next
day, she was playfully nipping at Amos again.
Willa and Ben volunteered to look after the
sweet chestnut horse. Taking care of her was
too fun to seem like a chore!

Willa couldn't believe it, but even her parents

agreed it was nice to have a horse in their field. "It feels right," Mom said on Friday morning as she looked out the kitchen window.

"Mmm-hmm," Dad murmured from behind the stove, where the final pot of chili was brewing. The carnival was the next day, and Dad wanted his chosen recipe's flavors "to blend and deepen overnight." Whatever that meant.

Willa and Ben thought it was funny that no one ever talked about how, in the process of taking in Buttercup, they had also adopted a puppy—a feisty, funny puppy who was happy to race in the field and sleep in the barn.

What everyone did want to talk about was the parade. Mr. Starling decided *not* to ride Buttercup. He wanted to give her time to recover. He did, however, agree to let Sarah ride Sweetums. "This way, I can walk right by your side," he told his daughter. "The parade can get kind of crazy."

Grandma Edna had said the exact same thing, and she had meant it. But she had been so impressed with how Willa and Ben had helped around the farm and cared for the ailing Buttercup, she was willing to make an exception. She told her grandkids they could ride in the parade too. Willa would be on Starbuck and Ben on Jake, and she would walk with them, just to be safe.

On the morning of parade day, Mom dropped the kids off at Miller Farm. They planned to put on their costumes in the barn and ride down to

Main Street. There, they would meet up with Sarah and her dad.

"We'll be watching for you near the carnival grounds," Mom reminded them. "Be careful and have fun!"

"Be careful and have fun" seemed like the slogan for the parade. It was what all the adults said to them, but Willa and Ben were not worried. First of all, Grandma Edna would be there. Second of all, Willa trusted Starbuck and Ben trusted Jake. They had both spent a lot of time with the horses to make sure the animals trusted them, too.

As they marched toward Main Street, Willa could not stop smiling. She was dressed like Annie Oakley, the famous sharpshooter from the Old West. Starbuck even looked a little like Annie's horse on the TV show. Ben was dressed like a Jedi Knight, with a long brown robe that covered his whole backside and most of Jake's, too.

Grandma made *tsk-tsk* sounds when she saw the crowd in front of the hardware store. "If you told me this time last year that I'd be leading my two grandkids in this mess, I never would have believed you," she said. Willa wor-

ried that Grandma might just turn them back around. Grandma was stubborn, but she was also a woman of her word. "I see Lloyd Starling over there. Let's go."

Sarah looked almost magical in her Glinda the Good Witch costume. She was excited to see Willa and Ben, but she was almost more excited to see Jasper Langely.

"Hey, Jasper," she called out. "Guess who owes me a Triple Fudge Caramel Brownie Surprise?"

Jasper tapped his finger to his chest. "Me," he said.

"Is that Wrangler?" Willa asked, looking at the horse Jasper was riding.

"No," he admitted. "My dad decided to ride Wrangler at the last second. This is Snacktime."

Willa nodded. The bay horse had long whiskers on her chin and a full round belly. "I like her name," Willa said genuinely. "It fits her."

"You're telling me," Jasper said, and he patted the horse's tummy. "She could eat two of those sundaes, no problem."

The local drum corps and brass band signaled the start of the parade with the song

"Seventy-Six Trombones." Ben could feel the beat of the drums in his chest. He sat tall on Jake's back. Willa gave Starbuck a reassuring pat and wrapped her fingers in the pony's coal-black mane.

The parade made its way right through the center of town. Both neighbors and strangers lined the streets, cheering and waving as the horses passed. Bunches of colorful balloons bobbed in the air, marking the parade path. Willa saw clowns, teenagers on stilts, and some women in long skirts on old-fashioned bicycles, but the ponies and horses were the real stars of the show.

As they neared the carnival grounds, Ben and Willa spotted their parents. Mom waved as Dad took pictures. Grandpa Reed was there.

Lena, Chipper, and the rest of the Starlings yelled from the crowd too.

Once they reached the end of the parade route, Grandma took Starbuck's and Jake's reins. "These two have done their job for the day," she said, feeding each an apple slice. "I'll take them home and then come back. You kids have fun. You've earned it."

Willa threw her arms around her grandma. "Thank you," she said into the sleeve of Grandma's jean jacket. "Thank you so much. This has been the best day I've had since we moved."

Grandma Edna put her hand on Willa's head. "Of course, dear."

"Thanks, Grandma," Ben said as he handed her his helmet. "It was fun."

Willa looked at her brother and rolled her eyes. "It was more than fun," she said. "It was *the best.*" She gave Starbuck a kiss, and they went off to find their friends.

After cotton candy, corn on the cob, and lemonade, they hardly had any room for chili. But they still went to the Greater Chincoteague Chili Cook-off booth.

Even though there were ten different chilis, Willa knew which one was her dad's. So did Lena. "It's the recipe with extra oregano," Lena said. "It was a good choice. I voted for him to win."

Willa did too.

When the winner of the chili contest announcement was made, the crowd wasn't surprised that Lena's father managed to win again.

"It's okay, Dad," Willa said as Mom pinned the red second-place ribbon on Dad's T-shirt. "Lena said Mr. Wise has a secret ingredient, and he uses it every year."

Dad sighed. "I figured as much," he said. "It tasted a little bit like chocolate. Maybe next year I should compete in the chowder cook-off instead."

Now Mom sighed and laughed. "At least we have a year to prepare," she said.

"Willa, Ben, come on!" The Dunlap kids looked up to see their friends pointing toward the Ferris wheel.

Willa, Sarah, and Lena sat together. Chipper and Ben were in the car just below. Willa drew in a deep breath, and she could smell the carnival: the horses, the chili, the funnel cakes, the salt from the ocean.

Once they were near the top, she could see all the way to their house. Buttercup was grazing in the field! She couldn't see New Cat or Amos, but she knew they were there, just as she knew the wild horses were over on Assateague.

It felt good. She reached out and took one of Sarah's and one of Lena's hands in hers. Willa was starting to believe her family belonged on the island, and their house was starting to be a real home—filled with people and animals that she loved. They really did feel like Chincoteague kids now.

Runaway Pony

♥

To Moochie and Wendy,

thank you

Chapter 1

FULL MOON FANCY. THE NAME SOUNDED MAGICAL. Willa let the words swirl in her head. She couldn't believe there was a new pony at Miller Farm.

"Just Fancy for short," Grandma Edna insisted. "No need for long, frilly names around here." When Grandma said "here," she meant the animal rescue center she ran. It was home to goats, chickens, rabbits, and especially ponies—Chincoteague ponies.

Ben and Willa hurried over to the small paddock to meet Fancy. "Where is she?" Ben wondered, glancing at his big sister. Willa searched the field.

"The small pasture's empty, Grandma," Willa called across the yard.

Grandma looked up. Her scowl pushed her eyebrows low. She stood up from her rosebushes. "Now don't tell me," she murmured. Grandma made her way over to where Willa and Ben stood. "Sure enough," she announced, examining the area. "We've got a pony to find. You two look on the other side of the house. I'll check behind the barn."

Before rushing off, Ben yanked a handful of

clover from the tall grass by the fence. "It's a peace offering," he said. "In case we find her." Willa nodded, amazed at how well her brother understood animals.

Even though Willa had taken riding lessons when they lived back in Chicago, she wouldn't have thought to grab a treat for the runaway pony. Ben had not really been around ponies or horses before they had moved to their new house on Chincoteague Island, but he had an easy way with them.

Now both kids were around horses and ponies every day. First, there was Buttercup. Buttercup belonged to their neighbors but was staying in the old barn at Ben and Willa's house for a while. Second, there were the horses at Grandma and Grandpa's place, Miller Farm. Of all those ponies, Willa and Ben shared a favorite: a sweet buckskin mare named Starbuck. Starbuck had arrived at the rescue center earlier that summer. At the time, her leg had been hurt. The kids had helped nurse Starbuck back to health, and now they loved her like their own.

But they couldn't think about Starbuck now. They had a lost pony to find!

"Grandma sounded mad," Ben remarked as they raced past the barn and the big pasture.

"She's probably just worried," Willa said as she rounded the corner of the one-story farmhouse. The grassy part of the yard was small but there was a deep wooded area in the back.

"We don't even know what Fancy looks like," Ben commented.

"Well, she's the one that's just roaming around, not in the pasture," Willa replied, swatting a bug away from her freckled nose. She squinted as she scanned the yard and trees. "I don't see her. Let's go to the garden."

Ben trudged behind his sister, glancing back over his shoulder. If he were a pony, where would he hide?

No luck in the garden. All they found was their grandma.

"I thought she'd be here too," Grandma Edna said. "It'd be just like that pony to make a feast of my carrots."

"Hey! What's going on?"

They looked up to see Lena and Clifton heading their way. Clifton was a teenager and often helped on the farm. His younger sister, Lena, sometimes tagged along. Willa was excited to see her friend.

"Lena, you have to help. There's a pony missing!" As Willa shared the details, Lena listened closely, twirling a finger around one of her many beaded braids.

"Let's first look for clues," Lena announced as soon as Willa was done. Together, Lena, Willa, and Ben went back to the small pasture. Clifton took the path through the woods. Grandma ran inside to recruit Grandpa. They would follow the fence along the far side of the barn, down toward the beach.

Lena moved quickly, but she did not rush. She carefully walked around the outside of the paddock fence. Next, she checked the closed gate and its latch. "Evidence!" she called out when she noticed a pile of manure.

"It's still steaming," Ben noted, his nose crinkled.

"That means it's fresh. Fancy can't have gone far," Lena determined. She shielded her eyes from the late-morning sun and turned a full circle. Willa and Ben searched too.

Willa frowned. It didn't make sense. Where was that new pony? If she couldn't have gone far, why hadn't they found her?

"Who's that?" Ben asked, pointing into the larger pasture area.

Willa's gaze fell on an unfamiliar pony, a shiny bay with a bushy mane and tail. The pony was standing right next to Starbuck. She had her head down and was busy ripping up tiny bites of grass.

Just then Grandma and Grandpa hurried out the farmhouse door. Grandpa had his keys, and Grandma held a lead rope.

"Grandma!" Willa called. "Is that her? Is that Fancy, grazing by Starbuck?"

"Well, I'll be," Grandma exclaimed. "How on earth did that mare find her way in there?"

It was a good question, but neither Grandma nor Grandpa attempted to answer it. Instead, they immediately headed for the gate and began to fiddle with the latch.

Willa, Ben, and Lena watched, confused.

"Do you think your grandma forgot she put Fancy in the main pasture?" Lena questioned.

"I doubt it," Willa answered. "Grandma never forgets anything."

"Especially not about the animals," Ben added. Grandma Edna had been a vet, and she prided herself in taking the best possible care of each and every creature at Miller Farm.

"Well, the fence looks too high for a pony to just jump over, and your grandparents are acting strange," Lena said. "I think there's something special about that new pony."

Willa knew Lena loved a mystery. Lena would turn anything into a whodunit, just so she could investigate. But, this time, Willa suspected her friend might be right.

"Let's go see what they're looking at," Lena suggested. The kids approached the entrance to the pasture quietly, curiously.

"What are you three doing here?" Grandma asked as soon as she noticed them. "Why don't you go for a walk down by the beach?"

Willa and Ben were happy to take their grandmother's suggestion. They loved to explore by the ocean, but even after they had arrived at the beach, Lena was certain they had been chased away on purpose. "Your grandparents are hiding something," she insisted.

"Don't be silly, Lena," Willa replied, curling

her long toes into the wet sand. "My grandparents have nothing to hide. They only want to take good care of the ponies." Willa was sure of that.

By the time their parents came to pick them up at the end of the day, Willa and Ben hardly remembered the earlier excitement of the escaped pony. The new excitement was that Dad was meeting Starbuck for the first time.

"So this is the pony I've heard so much about," Mr. Dunlap said. With a gentle nudge, Mom encouraged him to reach out his hand. Ben quickly put an apple slice on his dad's palm. After a few warm sniffs, Starbuck took the treat and crunched it happily. Dad had grown up in the city, so he didn't have much experience with horses.

"Isn't she great?" Willa asked, looking into the pony's warm brown eyes.

"She seems nice enough," Dad admitted.

"Starbuck's the best," Ben said, and he gave her another apple slice.

Chapter 2

BEN'S GOOD MOOD HAD DISAPPEARED BY THE next day. "When does school start?" he mumbled. When Ben was grumpy, all his words came out low and rumbly, running together.

"Next Tuesday," Mom answered as she pulled into a parking spot in front of Seacoast Elementary. "Aren't you excited?" Mom's voice was high and chirpy. Willa wondered if their mom was most excited of all.

Everyone got out and closed their doors. "This is exactly how they did it when I was a student here," Mom explained. "They would post the class lists on the front windows of the school." Willa and Ben rushed forward, but Mom lingered on the edge of the sidewalk.

Willa spotted the sheet for fifth grade immediately. As soon as she found her name, she scanned farther down the roster. Sarah Starling! Lena Wise!

"Willa!"

Willa turned around when she heard her name. "Sarah!" she yelled back to her friend, who had just arrived. "We're in the same class. Lena, too."

Sarah grabbed Willa's hand and pulled her

back to the windows to survey the list.

"Mr. McGory! He's supernice, and he has lots of animals in his room." Sarah gave Willa's hand a happy squeeze. Only then did the two delighted girls notice their less-than-thrilled brothers standing next to them.

Ben and Sarah's brother, Chipper, shared the same dismal expression. They did not have the same teacher.

"I got Ms. Hardy," Chipper moaned. He turned to Ben. "In case you wondered, her name fits her. She is *not* easy. You have Ms. Freeman. She is nice *and* funny."

"At least you'll know someone in your class," Ben complained back. "You are the only person I know in the whole school."

"Um, exaggerate much?" Sarah asked.

"You kind of know your sister . . . and me."

Ben's face scrunched up. Big sisters—and their friends—didn't count. Ben scooted closer to Chipper. Then he started whispering.

The moms had been talking near the parking lot, but they came toward the school entrance now.

"What are you two up to?" Mom asked with a coy expression when she saw Ben and Chipper.

"Nothing." The boys answered so quickly they gave themselves away. They were concocting a plan.

"Nothing big at least," Ben added.

The moms looked at each other and smiled.

"I like when school starts again," Mrs. Starling said.

"Me too," Willa and Ben's mom added. "Once

the kids are in class, I can get organized and really think about the inn."

"Your bed-and-breakfast!" Mrs. Starling exclaimed. "When's the grand opening?"

The Dunlaps had a big, old house, and they planned to use the extra bedrooms for guests—paying guests. There would be a restaurant, too.

"Not for a while," Mom admitted. It was taking longer than they had thought. "We just finished the website. We put it up so we could feel like the inn is a real thing, but we're still a far cry from being ready for business. Maybe later this fall."

Willa was listening to the parents' conversation. "Later this fall" sounded far away. Summer had been so nice, so carefree. No school, no real routine. Willa liked school, but she wished things didn't have to change.

"No way!"

Willa had never heard Mom use that phrase before. She exchanged glances with Ben between bites of spaghetti. They were the only ones at the big wooden dinner table. Mom and Dad claimed they were too distracted to eat.

"No way!" Mom repeated.

"You're the one who wanted to put up the website," Dad said, shaking his head. "You said it would make the inn seem 'real.'"

"I didn't think someone would book a room in the first twenty-four hours." Mom was pacing now, striding from one side of the kitchen island to the other. She stared at the laptop on the counter. She glared at it as if it were a bully who had played a mean trick.

Dad slouched on a stool and watched Mom go back and forth. His eyebrows were up, but the corners of his mouth turned down.

"It's so soon!" Mom continued. "We still need to paint the downstairs bathroom, and clean out all that stuff behind the barn."

Willa and Ben looked at each other. Mom was just getting started. She always rattled off long lists of things to do. "And put up towel hooks, and—"

"We can do this," Dad announced, interrupting the list.

"We can?" Mom questioned.

"Of course," Dad said, slapping his hand on the counter. He was sitting up nice and straight now. "It's just one weekend. We don't need to have the restaurant up and running. We don't have to have every detail in place."

"You're right," Mom replied. "Just the one room, and then a nice breakfast."

"Yes. A bed and a breakfast," Dad confirmed. "That's it."

Mom and Dad both sighed.

Willa and Ben both took deep breaths. To them, it sounded like a lot.

Chapter 3

"I'M NOT SURE YOU'RE OLD ENOUGH FOR THAT," Mom said, putting a stack of dirty breakfast dishes in the sink. It was the next day, and Willa was trying to make the most of the end of summer vacation.

"But it would be so much fun," Willa insisted. "Maybe Grandma would let Sarah ride Fancy; then we could take a picnic down to the dunes. I'll bet Starbuck would love it."

"It sounds lovely, but I don't think your grandma would let you girls go off on your own with two ponies, especially two ponies she doesn't know that well. Grandma would feel too responsible if something went wrong."

"What could go wrong?" As soon as the words slipped out of her mouth, Willa wanted to take them back. She knew you could not plan for everything, especially when animals were involved.

"Besides, you can't just go off and leave your brother."

"Ben could hang out with Chipper," Willa suggested. "He doesn't like to ride as much as I do." Willa was pretty sure of that. Ben seemed to enjoy just being *around* the animals.

She noticed a pad of paper on the table across from her. "What's this?" she asked, reaching for it.

"It's our to-do list," Mom answered.

"Wow, you actually wrote it all down," Willa commented. "Instead of just announcing everything at dinner. That's good, Mom." Willa had always believed in lists herself.

"Yes, if we are going to have other people in our home, we have to get serious, get organized," Mom said. "For starters, you and your brother can't leave your stuff down here."

"Okay," Willa said.

"It has to go in your room, first thing after you get home from school."

That made sense. "I'll make sure Ben does it too."

"Great. Your dad and I really need your help."

"Okay," Willa said again. She wasn't sure how their conversation had changed. It had started with her talking about taking ponies for a picnic on the beach, and it had ended with Mom handing her and Ben a basket of clean clothes to put away and talk of even more chores. Summer was definitely coming to an end.

"Really?" Ben asked when Willa passed on the news later that day. He kicked the toe of his sneaker in the sandy driveway dirt. "We never had to keep our school stuff in our rooms in Chicago."

"We never ran an inn in Chicago either."

Ben turned toward the old white house. He looked way up to where the guest rooms were, on the third floor. "Do you really think Mom and Dad can do this?"

Willa looked up too, her eyes squinting against the sun. "Yes, I do. Mom made a real list this time. On paper."

Ben's eyebrows shot up. A real list.

"And they didn't give us any crazy jobs, like cleaning out all the weeds behind the barn. We got easy chores, like being in charge of Amos after school."

"But what about all our other chores? Will we still be able to go to Miller Farm?" Ben asked.

Willa bit her lip. She was worried about that too. They had to make it to the farm to visit Starbuck.

Willa and Ben had taken on a number of chores over the summer. They helped care for Buttercup by cleaning her stall. They were responsible for feeding Amos, the adorable black-and-white puppy who was Buttercup's best friend. Willa and Ben also took care of New

Cat, who was in charge of mouse control. There were other jobs that didn't have anything to do with animals, but those were not nearly as much fun. Those jobs did, however, take time. "We'll have to do our chores first thing when we get home, then head straight to the farm. And we'll have to take Amos with us."

"If we take Amos, we have to walk. That'll take *forever*! He's always sniffing." Ben was right, the puppy hardly took three steps without stopping to smell something.

"I have a plan," Willa reassured him.

For the next half hour, Willa and Ben searched through the barn for supplies. Mom and Dad used part of the old red barn for storage. Plus, there were lots of things left from the previous owners. The kids had spent a lot of time in the

Our To-do List

Buttercup

- ☐ Clean stalls
- ☐ Brush
- ☐ Fresh Hay
- ☐ Water
- ☐ Paddock morning

Amos

- ☐ Food
- ☐ Walk & play ball
- ☐ Puppy training

New Cat

- ☐ Food
- ☐ Water
- ☐ Chin scratch

building. They were the ones who had cleared out the stalls, just in case. Thanks to them, Buttercup was able to come stay at Misty Inn when he had become sick. Buttercup was great, but there were two stalls, and Willa and Ben hoped that one day the other one would belong to a certain special pony.

"I couldn't find a straw basket," Ben told Willa. "Only this old crate."

"That's fine. This isn't *The Wizard of Oz*," Willa said, examining the plastic crate to check the size. "We just need some cardboard on the bottom so his legs don't poke through."

"And a blanket, so he's comfy. Or he'll jump out."

Willa studied her brother's face. She thought it was funny that he could think of that, but he couldn't remember to put on clean underwear unless someone told him.

"Look! I'll bet this crate was used as a bike basket before." Willa pointed to where a bracket and some screws hung from one of the crate's corners. That setup made it easier. Willa held the crate in place while Ben tightened the screws.

All the hard work was worthwhile. Amos loved the crate. As soon as Ben plopped him inside, he smelled the soft green blanket and woofed happily. Then, when Willa put her weight on the bike pedals and started riding, Amos placed his front paws on the edge and yipped for joy. Willa pedaled as carefully as she could. It was hard not to laugh, the way Amos's tongue dangled from his mouth.

"That's one problem solved," Willa announced after their quick ride around the neighborhood. "Now we can take Amos with us when we go to the farm."

"So we can still see Starbuck," Ben concluded. "Good."

It was good. Their grandmother was very
practical about the ponies at the rescue center. Starbuck's leg was totally healed. The pony
didn't need to stay at the rescue center any-

more. If Grandma Edna decided it was time to find Starbuck a new home, Grandma would do it. When she made up her mind, that was that. But the Dunlap kids wouldn't give up their favorite pony without a fight.

Chapter 4

"I DON'T KNOW HOW I FORGOT ABOUT IT," MOM said, sounding concerned, nervous, and guilty all at once.

"Don't worry, Mom. We'll be fine." Willa handed her mother a notebook, which she placed in her small suitcase. It was the Friday before school started, and Mom had remembered just the day before that she had to go on a trip.

"I signed up for this bed-and-breakfast conference months ago. I had no idea I'd miss your first day of school." She looked up at Willa as she zipped her bag. "Sorry, sweetie."

"It's fine. There will be lots of school days," Willa said.

"When did you get so grown-up?" Mom asked. She sounded sad.

Willa was the most organized one in the family. Everyone knew that, so it wasn't a surprise that Mom had told her she'd need to help Dad. "You know he's not good at getting you guys out the door in the morning," she said.

"Don't worry," Willa assured her.

"Make sure you and Ben are ready for the bus. Be at the mailbox by eight o' clock."

"We will be," Willa assured her again. They

heard the doorbell. "That must be Grandma."

"She's always early," Mom said. "Especially for the airport." She tugged her bag behind her.

Everyone came down to see Mom off. She gave them all hugs. "Take care of one another," she ordered. "And no more tardies."

Mom looked right at Willa when she said that.

Willa elbowed Ben.

Dad just smiled. "Learn lots about bed-and-breakfasts," he said. "Our guests will be here before you know it."

Mom blew a kiss and ducked into the car. Grandma Edna waved and backed out of the driveway.

"What should we do now?" Dad asked blankly.

Willa sighed. She was going to be busy while Mom was gone.

On the morning of the first day of school, Willa woke to a horrible clanging. "Did Dad get a new alarm?" she mumbled as she pushed herself out of bed. The clanging grew louder. The house seemed to rattle and shake. Willa stumbled out of her room and followed the sound. It led her upstairs, to one of the guest bedrooms. Her dad was there, kneeling in front of an old metal contraption, which was hissing.

"What's going on?" Willa cried over the noise.

"I think the radiator is broken," he said. "It got cold last night, so I turned on the heat."

A spray of steam sputtered from the pipe. "Watch out!" Dad yelled. "It could burn you."

They stood at a distance and stared at the noisy, drippy, feisty radiator.

"No showers this morning," Dad announced. "This is an old house, and I think the heat and the plumbing are connected."

"All right," Willa said, heading downstairs to wake Ben, who had managed to sleep through the racket.

"You should avoid all plumbing," Dad called from the third floor. "Don't even use the sink."

The morning routine was tricky without running water. Willa and Ben had to brush their teeth with water from the pitcher in the fridge. Willa used that to wash off the apples for their lunches too. Things took longer. Before they knew it, they were running late for the bus.

"Hurry!" Willa insisted, zipping her lunch box.

Ben grabbed his backpack and rushed to the door.

Dad appeared at the top of the stairs with a mop and a bucket. A stream dribbled down from the top step. "Have a great first day, kids!" He was smiling and looking hopeful, despite his soggy pajama pants.

"Do you need help?" Willa asked. "Should we stay?"

"No. Everything will be fine," he said. He held the mop up straight with one hand and saluted with the other.

Willa laughed as she took Ben's hand and ran out the door. They could see the bus from the front porch. "Go!" Willa yelled, and Ben leaped ahead. He made it to the mailbox just as the yellow bus's door folded open. Willa came up behind him. By the time Chipper and Sarah got on at the next stop, Willa had caught her breath.

Sarah slid in beside her. Chipper sat with Ben. Willa sighed. They had made it! Even without Mom. Even with a crazy radiator leak. Even without running water. She was relieved . . . and certain the rest of the day would be a breeze after that.

Then the bus jolted to a stop.

"Well, I never," the bus driver proclaimed. He scratched his graying whiskers and stared out the front window.

Sarah stood up to look out. "Oh no!" she exclaimed. "Willa!"

As soon as Willa stood up, she gulped.

There, in the middle of the road, was Starbuck.

Chapter 5

WILLA RACED TO THE FRONT OF THE BUS. "I know that pony. I have to get off," she declared.

"Nothing doing, missy," the bus driver said. "I can't let anyone off. Only at school or your stop. It's a rule."

"But someone might hit her. She could get hurt."

Now Ben was standing next to her. "Please, mister," he begged.

"I'm sorry, but it's my job to get you to school safely," he said. "Can't let no runaway pony get in the way." The bus driver leaned his head and shoulder out the narrow window. "Move along now," he called.

The buckskin pony did not move, so he honked the horn.

"Starbuck, get out of the road. It's not safe," Willa pleaded, though not loud enough for her favorite pony to hear.

The bus driver honked again. All the kids on the bus were now standing and yelling.

For a moment Starbuck stood her ground. She seemed unfazed. She faced the bus head-on, lazily flicking an ear and swishing her tail.

"Go on, girl," Willa whispered.

Starbuck pricked her ears forward. She tossed her head in the air and whinnied. Then, slowly, she made her way to the side of the road and stopped there.

"That's a good horse," the bus driver said, easing the bus back into gear.

Willa and Ben scurried to the back row of seats and watched out the window. Starbuck didn't move. She just got smaller as the bus drove away. Brother and sister pushed themselves against the glass to catch the last glimpse of her. Willa felt trapped. They had to do something! How had Starbuck gotten out? Where was she going? And how would she get back home?

"I've got my walkie-talkie," Ben said hopefully, but then he remembered Chipper had the other one in the front of the bus. It was part of their master plan to keep in touch, even though they had different teachers.

"We couldn't have used it to call Dad anyway," Willa said, flopping around to sit down. "The house is flooding."

Sarah was waiting at the bus door. As soon as Willa stepped to the ground, Sarah's hand was on her shoulder. "We'll go straight to the office. Ms. Parker will help us."

Willa told Ben to go with Chipper, so the other boy could show him where his class would be. "I promise to let you know as soon as I hear anything." She bent down to look into her brother's eyes. He nodded, but didn't say a word.

Sarah led Willa into the office of Seacoast Elementary. It looked a lot like the office at

Willa's old school in Chicago. Willa had gone there whenever she was late and had to check in.

A woman with cat earrings and long, hot-pink-painted fingernails looked up from the front desk. "Sarah Starling," she said. "Welcome back."

Sarah smiled, introduced Ms. Parker to Willa, and explained the situation. When Sarah was done, Ms. Parker sent her on to class. Willa looked at the clock. It was already 8:18. School started at 8:20. She had given Mom her word: no more tardies.

"Don't you worry," Ms. Parker said. "I'll take you to class. Your teacher won't count you late." She picked up a phone with a long curly cord. "Go ahead and call your grandma. She'll know just what to do."

When Willa hung up the phone, she felt a little better. Grandma Edna was leaving right away to track down Starbuck. She had said she'd call Sarah's mom to help too.

"Your grandma is something else," Ms. Parker said. "My Patsy refuses to go to any other vet." When Willa looked closer at Ms. Parker's desk, she noticed a collection of picture frames. All featured photos of a large black-and-white cat.

"Grandma's pretty great," Willa agreed.

Ms. Parker told stories about Patsy as she walked Willa to class. When Willa opened the door to Room 24, all heads turned to her. Normally, Willa would have been embarrassed, but she quickly located Sarah's and Lena's friendly faces. She forced a smile when Mr. McGory pointed to an empty desk. She sat down and tried to pay attention, but she could not stop thinking about Starbuck.

Just before lunch, there was a knock on the classroom door. It was Ms. Parker. She had a piece of folded pink paper in her hand. "A message for Willa Dunlap," she said.

Whispers flitted all around as Willa opened the note.

Your grandma called to say Starbuck is safe back at Miller Farm. You can visit her later. I let your brother know too.
Ms. P.

She had drawn a cat face next to her name.

♥

Starbuck's escape was big news at the lunch table. "It's not a coincidence," Lena insisted.

"What does that mean?" Sarah asked as she opened her sandwich tin.

"Two ponies and two escapes in two weeks?" Lena said, waving her pretzel rod in the air. "They have to be connected. I suspect foul play."

"You always suspect foul play," Sarah retorted.

"I agree that it's weird," Willa said. She was still too nervous to eat. "But I don't think anyone is letting them loose on purpose."

"Maybe not," Lena admitted. "But why do you think Starbuck wandered so far from the farm? The other pony didn't do that."

Willa had been wondering the same thing.

"Maybe Starbuck wants to be free," Sarah suggested, "to go back to Assateague."

Willa turned to her friend, horrified. She never would have thought of that. The very idea hurt Willa's feelings.

Sarah didn't seem to notice. "Remember how Phantom, Misty's mother, swam back to Assateague to be with the wild herd?"

Of course Willa remembered. Willa had read the famous book about Misty several times by now. She was fascinated by the fact that wild ponies lived on Assateague Island, a thin sliver of land that lay between Chincoteague and the open sea. "But Phantom had been wild for a long time," Willa argued. "Starbuck hasn't lived on Assateague since she was a foal. Her old owners told us so."

Sarah shrugged. "It looked like she was going somewhere. I was just trying to figure out where."

Willa didn't have a reply. She was so fond of Starbuck. She wanted the pony to be happy. Willa hoped she wasn't running away from Miller Farm.

Chapter 6

IT HARDLY FELT LIKE THE SAME DAY WHEN they arrived home after school. They soon found their dad on the third floor. Willa was relieved that he wasn't still in his pajamas, but his jeans and T-shirt were sopping wet.

"How was your day?" he asked.

"Anything but typical," Willa said. Ben agreed with a firm nod of his head.

"Mine was about the same," Dad replied. "Homework?"

"A little," Willa replied. "I can do it after dinner." Ben nodded again.

"What did you think about the other kids? Did you meet anyone new?"

"Kind of," Willa answered. A picture of Ms. Parker, with her nails and old-fashioned phone, popped into her head. But the secretary wasn't a kid! "I mostly hung out with Sarah and Lena."

"Ben?" Dad asked.

"Same," was Ben's answer. Willa noticed his hand move to touch the walkie-talkie hanging from his belt. She felt bad that Ben and Chipper weren't in homeroom together. It wasn't easy making brand-new friends.

Even though Willa had been nervous about

the first day—new school, new kids, new challenges—that had all gone smoothly compared to the Great Starbuck Escape fiasco.

Willa noticed a stack of dry rags right next to a pile of wet ones.

"Do you need help?" she offered, even though she had hoped they'd be able to go to the farm.

"Not really," Dad said, surveying the puddle that surrounded the radiator. "Your grandfather came by with one of his friends who is a plumber. He fixed the leak. I just have to clean up now." He sloshed the mop back in a rubber bucket. "Besides, I think you two might want to check in on that pony Starbuck. I'm sure you want to get the rest of the story from Grandma."

"Yes, yes!" Willa's face brightened. She reached to hug her dad with both arms, but he tried to pull away.

"I'm all wet, sweetheart," he said. "You've got your good school clothes on." Willa squeezed tighter. She was sometimes surprised how adults didn't think about what really mattered. Her clothes could always go in the wash.

❤

Dad fixed them a huge after-the-first-day-of-school snack. They filled him in on the thrilling bus ride and all the events that had followed. He gave them a play-by-play of how the radiator sounded when it started to spout water like a fountain. Ben almost choked on his cheese and crackers. Their dad could be pretty silly when he wanted.

"You sure you have enough energy to ride to your grandparents'?" Dad asked.

Willa and Ben were sure. Amos was too. The puppy yipped happily as Ben placed him in the carrier on the front of Willa's bike. Ben lingered there, scratching Amos behind the ears. "You think she's okay?"

It took Willa a moment to realize what her brother was asking. "Starbuck is fine," she answered. "Grandma would have let us known if something had happened. She'd have told Grandpa to tell Dad, then Dad would have told us." Willa knew that much for certain, but she had other concerns. What if Starbuck was trying to get free, like Sarah had said? What if Grandma decided the beautiful buckskin was too much trouble and needed to go to a new home right away? Willa didn't have answers to those questions, so she rode her very fastest to Miller Farm. Ben struggled to keep up.

When they arrived, Starbuck trotted over right away. The pony looked as good as new. Maybe better.

Willa lifted Amos from the crate, and the puppy waddled right into the field. He touched noses with Starbuck, his tail wagging like a windup toy. Then he moved on to make friends with Fancy. He ran between the two ponies, making figure eights, stopping from time to time to give them each a sniff. He often did the same thing to Buttercup, back home.

Ben reached his arm over the top rail of the wooden fence and stroked Starbuck's velvety ears. The pony's eyelids fluttered closed. She looked peaceful. "Maybe she wasn't trying to run away," Ben suggested. "Maybe she was trying to find us."

Willa took a deep breath and gazed at her little brother. She had been thinking the same thing—hoping the same thing—but she didn't dare put the thought into words.

"I think she could track us down," Ben continued. "I think she's that smart."

All of a sudden, Grandma Edna was right behind them. She had appeared out of nowhere. "Smart? There's nothing smart about getting loose. Starbuck could have been hit by a car out there. The road is never a safe place for a horse, and it was rush hour."

Willa had to hide her smirk. Compared to the city, Chincoteague had no rush hour on its roads. But she still got Grandma's point. They were lucky Starbuck was back at Miller Farm, safe and sound. "Thank you, Grandma," Willa said. "For going to get her. We were so worried."

"I was worried too. It was definitely out of character for that pony."

As they spoke, Fancy ambled up next to Starbuck. Fancy gave a low nicker of greeting to Starbuck. Starbuck nickered back to the shiny bay. Then Fancy put her head over the fence, hoping to get a pet as well.

"Now, Starbuck, you'd best be careful in choosing your companions," Grandma advised. Willa recognized that tone. It had a hint of disapproval. Willa wondered what Grandma Edna

was trying to say. Did she question whether Starbuck and Fancy should be friends? That seemed odd. Ben was glancing back and forth, from Grandma to the two ponies. He was trying to figure it out as well.

Willa told herself that it couldn't hurt to ask. "What do you mean, Grandma?"

"I mean that we can't have Starbuck picking up any bad habits. Especially not now. She's good and healthy again, so we should be finding her a new home." Grandma stepped forward and gave Starbuck a steady pat on the neck. "You be good now, you hear?" she said to the buckskin pony.

Hearing Grandma mention a new home for Starbuck rattled Willa. She was so flustered that she barely heard what Grandma said next.

It was something about how Grandpa had driven to the hardware store to buy a new latch for the pasture gate. "Can't have any more escape antics," she murmured as she headed to the barn.

It was hard to settle down and think about homework after all the excitement of the day. Even though they were in different classes and different grades, Willa and Ben had the same assignment. They had to write a personal essay about what they had done during the summer. So much had happened! Where would they even start?

Chapter 7

A FEW DAYS PASSED WITHOUT ANY DRAMA AT the Dunlap house. Both kids made it to the bus stop on time, and the bus didn't make any unexpected stops for animals in the middle of the road. The radiator in the upstairs bedroom was fixed, and everyone could take showers again. Mom came back home. She was more excited than ever about the family's plan for a bed-and-breakfast, which was good. The inn's first guests were coming in less than a week!

Things were going well at Miller Farm, too. Even though Grandpa couldn't find the exact latch he had wanted at the hardware store, no ponies had escaped from the field. Grandpa had ordered the new, improved latch, and any day it would arrive in the mail. For now, Grandma and Grandpa used a whole roll of twine to tie the gate shut at night.

But all the knots in the twine made it hard to get the gate open again, and that's just what Willa wanted to do. She, Ben, and Grandma were going on a ride together to celebrate the end of the first week of school. As usual, Willa would ride Starbuck. Ben would ride the big sweetheart Jake, who was an honest-to-goodness real draft horse. The surprise was that instead of walking alongside the horses, Grandma Edna was going to ride too. Even more unexpected was the fact that she intended to ride the new pony, Fancy.

"This pony needs to get out and about," the retired vet said as she pulled herself into the saddle. "Otherwise, she makes plans of her own."

Willa turned around in her saddle and locked eyes with Ben. Ben raised his eyebrows. There Grandma went again, with her mysterious statements. Willa and Ben had attempted to figure them out, but they hadn't had much luck. For now, Grandma said nothing more. She never gave them more than a hint.

From the various murmurs and comments,

Willa and Ben were fairly certain that Grandma Edna blamed Fancy for both escapes, but they didn't know why. As far as they knew, Starbuck was the only pony that had left the farm when the gate was open on the first day of school.

Grandpa Reed wasn't helping them get to the bottom of things either. They had asked him specific questions, but he had not given them specific answers.

Both kids listened closely as they rode along the windy beach with their grandmother. She seemed to be having a conversation with Fancy, but her words were too hushed to understand. To make it even harder to hear, Amos let out giddy barks at a steady beat. The puppy loved being near the horses, and he couldn't help announcing his joy to everyone.

From this stretch of Chincoteague, the wild island of Assateague did not look very far away. It reminded Willa of what Sarah had said. Was it possible that Starbuck wanted to be free again? It pained Willa to think of it. Part of her heart belonged to Starbuck. She wanted the pony to be close to her . . . and Ben.

After a long walk along the beach, they were nearing the farm again. "I dropped my walkie-talkie!" Ben called out as soon as he realized it was missing. "I had it at the start. I swear."

Willa's tummy was already rumbling for dinner. She couldn't imagine having to go back and search for her brother's tech gear. "Why did you take a walkie-talkie on a horseback ride?" she asked, annoyed. He insisted on taking that thing *everywhere.*

"It might have come in handy," he replied.

"Well, a walkie-talkie would be handy now, so we could call someone to go look for it," Willa mumbled.

"Now, children," Grandma Edna began, and they were certain she was about to scold them both, but she was interrupted by a faint jingle. It was a tinkling sound that was growing louder by the second. Soon, it was joined by jolly panting.

"It's Amos!" Ben called. "He has my walkie-talkie!" The puppy was bounding up behind them, his collar clattering with each stride. His sharp puppy teeth clenched Ben's gadget, the antenna sticking up in the air.

"Well, thank goodness," Grandma said. "That pup can track down anything. On Monday he

dug up one of my gardening gloves. I thought it was gone for good."

Amos stopped next to Starbuck, and the pony reached down to nuzzle the puppy. "She's thanking him," Ben noted. The puppy raised his nose and licked Starbuck's muzzle. "They're friends."

Willa was relieved. Between the long school day, the chores at home, and fun at the farm, she was hungry and exhausted. It was good that Amos had found the walkie-talkie. He was earning his keep—and his bike rides.

The topic of the runaway ponies came up again at dinner that night. "Lena thinks that Fancy is some kind of escape artist," Willa shared. "She thinks Fancy is the one who let Starbuck out, that maybe Fancy can pick locks. Remember how she got from one field to the other when both gates were closed?"

"Does Grandma Edna have a secret?" Ben wondered out loud. "Why won't she tell us what is going on? Is it because we're kids?" A pout appeared on Ben's face as he asked the last question.

Mom looked at Dad before she answered. "I don't think Grandma is trying to keep anything from you, at least not on purpose. You know, she often thinks of those horses and ponies like they're family, so she tries not to say mean things about them." Mom lifted a flowered napkin to wipe the corners of her mouth. "And she's never been one to start rumors."

"Rumors about a pony?" Ben said, swallowing a giggle.

"Grandma Edna doesn't like gossip," Mom stated. "She thinks it's a waste of time."

"Well, she's said a whole lot about Fancy," Willa explained. "But it's all under her breath. We can't hear a single word."

"Maybe you'll be able to figure it out next week, when you stay there," Dad suggested.

Mom had planned a lot of last-minute projects for the inn. Dad had suggested that it might be easier for the kids to stay at their grandparents' while the work was being done. As soon as it was complete, the first guests would arrive at the bed-and-breakfast. Willa and Ben would stay over at Grandma and Grandpa's then, too.

Part of Willa was sad to miss the first visitors at Misty Inn. But she knew she and Ben would have fun at Miller Farm. The best part was that Grandma couldn't send Starbuck to a new home while Willa and Ben were staying there . . . at least not if they had anything to say about it!

Chapter 8

FROM THE BEGINNING, MOM AND DAD HAD SAID that the inn would be a Dunlap Family Adventure. Willa had thought that it would be like the time they drove the car all the way to the Grand Canyon. But the inn felt bigger than the Grand Canyon, if that was possible. Every day there was another closet to clean out, a new paint color to pick, a new recipe to taste. It was a lot, but no project felt bigger than trying to move all the furniture in the house into the kitchen.

"This chair is heeea-vy," Ben groaned, his fingers burning from the weight. Willa could feel the muscles in her arms stretching and straining.

"Kids, kids, put that down," Dad advised, swooping in to help them lower the chair's base. "It's too heavy."

"But there's only heavy stuff left," Willa said.

"Then it'll have to wait for your mom and me," said Dad. "Or the workers tomorrow morning." After the leak on the third floor dribbled all the way down the stairs, the wood floors were splotchy and stained. Mom wanted them to shine. While the floors were being refinished, all the furniture needed to be some-where else. It was a big job.

Dad took a quick survey of their progress and then collapsed onto the chair, right where they'd dropped it in the middle of the hallway. "You should go pack, and then I'll take you to the farm," he said, resting his eyes. "You guys are lucky you'll get a break from this place."

Willa felt bad for her dad. He was a chef. He had always been excited about the restaurant side of the inn, but lately he and Mom had been thinking about everything else. Handmade quilts. Fancy brass doorknobs. Online reser-vations. Antique lamps. "There are only two people coming to the inn, right?" Willa said. "It doesn't have to be perfect."

Dad sighed. "When you get older, you'll realize

that in real life, there is no such thing as perfect," he said, his eyes still closed. "But when your mother's involved, it has to be pretty darn close."

Life at Miller Farm seemed much more calm. Even though the kids were spending several nights, Grandma Edna planned to stick to her usual routine. "I'll put you to work," she said. Willa and Ben were happy to help out, especially when it came to tending to Jake and the ponies.

The very first night, they started by mucking manure from the field. Unlike at Misty Inn, the horses and ponies at the rescue center spent the night outside. "More like in the wild," Grandma Edna had insisted as she slung a shovelful into the wheelbarrow. Together the three finished in no time.

"You don't have to tie it so tight," Ben said as Willa wound the twine around the gate several times for good measure. "Even if Fancy bites through the twine and opens the gate, Starbuck won't go anywhere. She'll see us go into the house tonight, and she'll know we are here. She doesn't need to try to find us. Right, girl?" Starbuck, who had been staying close to the kids all evening, heaved a snuffled sigh. "See? She agrees," Ben declared.

Ever since Starbuck stopped the bus on the first day of school, Ben had decided that she had been looking for them. He believed it was the only explanation. "She wanted to find us," Ben said. "You and me."

He was even more convinced the next morning, when all was well in the field. Starbuck, Fancy, Jake, Annie, and every other pony was quietly grazing in the early sun. They were all there when Willa and Ben came home from school as well.

The second week of school had been good for both of them. Sarah and Lena had introduced Willa to several kids, and Willa had started to pick up on Mr. McGory's humor. He was funny! Best of all, Willa had noticed Ben laughing with a group of boys in his gym class. Ben and Chipper still carried their walkie-talkies everywhere, but at least Ben was starting to open up to other kids as well.

"Finally got the right latch," Grandpa announced as the kids walked up the long driveway on Friday afternoon, "so we don't have to deal with that prickly twine anymore." This was good news to Willa, because the twine made her fingers red and itchy. Even better, she wouldn't have to worry about Starbuck getting out anymore. That was one less reason for Grandma Edna to insist on finding a new home for the pony.

That evening the sky was a deep shade of purple. Willa and Ben hoped that all was going well with their parents at home. The first guests should have arrived at Misty Inn. Willa hoped they were enjoying the sunset and all the wonder of being on Chincoteague Island.

At Miller Farm the pastures seemed to be filled with a lavender mist. To Willa and Ben, it felt almost magical, getting to feed Starbuck fresh carrots from the garden just before bed-time. They were in their pajamas and barn boots. It was a funny combination, but it felt good. It felt special.

Both kids were happy to have Buttercup staying in their barn at home, but Butter-cup was not their horse. She belonged to the Starlings, Sarah and Chipper's family. It was different being on Miller Farm at night, spend-ing these lazy hours with Starbuck. Willa and Ben loved Starbuck as if she were their own.

Saying good night to the pony was easier when they knew they would see her first thing in the morning. Even Amos, who usually whim-pered whenever they had to leave the farm, seemed more at ease. Maybe it was because he was allowed to sleep inside when the kids stayed at their grandparents' house. At Misty Inn, he always slept in the barn.

"Sweet dreams, Starbuck," Willa said, turning the latch on the new lock. Ben petted the pony's muzzle and double-checked the gate. Willa picked up Amos and blew Starbuck one last kiss before heading inside for the night.

Willa went to sleep smiling, but she woke up a few hours later. Amos was whining even though his eyes were closed. The puppy had awakened Ben, too. "Poor little guy. He must be having a bad dream," Willa said. Ben rested his hand on Amos's side, and the pup quieted down.

But his whimpers returned a few hours later. "What should we do?" Ben asked as the whining grew louder. The kids' grandparents were sleeping in the next room, and they didn't dare disturb them.

"Maybe we should wake him up," she suggested, but she wasn't certain. "It might stop the dream, and he can go back to sleep."

Both kids crawled out of bed and sat next to Amos. As soon as Ben gave him a shake, the puppy jolted awake. He stopped whining but started barking. Sharp, insistent barks.

"Shhhhh." Willa tried to soothe him, but Amos did not want to be soothed. He jumped up, bolted to the bedroom door, and nudged it open. They could hear his collar jingle as he darted through the house.

"He probably needs to go out," Willa said, grabbing her barn boots. Amos wasn't used to being cooped up all night. "We can let him go to the bathroom and bring him right back in." Ben was just a step behind her. They tried to tiptoe as they ran. They found Amos waiting with his cold nose pressed against the door.

The puppy bounded outside and raced toward the front yard. His barks were louder than they had ever been. He sounded excited and afraid. As soon as they rounded the corner, Willa and Ben knew why. The field gate was wide open, and Starbuck was gone.

Chapter 9

"I TRIPLE-CHECKED THE LOCK," BEN DECLARED.

"I know," Willa said. "I'm not blaming you. Remember, I'm the one who locked it in the first place." They both stared at the field. The night air was thick and wet. Even through the haze, the kids could tell that the pasture was full, except for the one pony they wanted to see most.

Willa stepped forward and relocked the gate. "That's not important now. What's important is finding Starbuck." She glanced around anxiously. "Oh no. Where's Amos?"

First the kids checked the barn. No Amos.

"He's probably one step ahead of us," Ben replied. "He's probably searching for a trail."

Slowly, Willa followed her brother's thinking. She realized that Amos had known all along. Even in his sleep, the puppy had suspected something was wrong. "We have to find him," she said.

Ben straightened up and looked around. The morning was still. "I think I hear him. Behind the house."

Brother and sister rushed to find the puppy, their bare feet loose in their boots. "Amos," Willa

called in a breathy whisper when they reached the backyard. Amos bounded forward with a yip. He stopped when he reached Willa, and sat down. "That's weird," she said. "He never sits."

Next, the puppy looked longingly into the woods. He sniffed the air, raised one paw, and whimpered.

While the sky around the house was starting to brighten to a dull gray, the wooded area was still dark and moody. "What do you think?" Willa asked.

"I think Amos is good at finding things. Grandma's glove. My walkie-talkie." As he spoke, he touched his hand to the gadget, which was dangling from the waistband of his plaid pajama pants. "And Starbuck," he added hopefully.

The puppy sniffed the air again.

"Okay, Amos," Willa said, ruffling the black patch of fur on his back. "Help us find her."

The puppy turned and trotted toward a gap in the trees. He stopped and smelled, then glanced back. "We're coming," Willa told him, but the shadows were daunting. Once they were under the trees, Willa could barely make out the path ahead of her. "Watch out," she warned Ben. "There are wet leaves on the ground. They're slippery."

Their eyes slowly adjusted, but Willa found she used her hearing more to pick up on Amos's cues: his sniffs, his pants, the upbeat jingle of his collar. He had run ahead, and she caught glimpses of his white tail only now and then.

The moist air clung to her skin, attracting a

chill. She didn't know if her goose bumps were from the cold or her concern.

"I don't get why she left," Ben said after a while. "She knew we were right there. Right in the farmhouse."

Without even looking, Willa could picture the pout on her brother's face. She felt the same way. Why did Starbuck escape? Could Sarah have been right? Did Starbuck want to be free? Willa knew that the wild horses swam the channel from Assateague every year for the pony auction. If Starbuck had made it across the water as a foal, she could certainly do it now as a full-grown pony. What if Amos wasn't on the right path? What if Starbuck was headed for the water? Willa worried that she and Ben might not see their favorite pony again.

Ben kept his eyes focused on Willa's boots. They were yellow and caught the small amount of light that seeped through the trees' leaves. He had to make sure to duck under low limbs, and push branches out of the way. Once, he tripped over a thick root. He hadn't even been able to see it! He wondered how Starbuck could pick her way through these dim woods. And why? The muddy ground was slick. There weren't any appealing patches of grass to eat. She should have just stayed back at Miller Farm. It didn't make any sense.

As Amos and the kids made their way, bird chirps began to announce the morning. Willa could hear the rev of car engines starting up. It was Saturday, so there wouldn't be a lot of traffic, but it didn't make Willa worry less.

There were still plenty of dangers for a lost pony.

Even though they were new to Chincoteague, Ben thought he knew the island fairly well. They had ridden their bikes all over that summer. They had explored the sandy stretches of beach. But Ben had no idea where they were now. At times, it seemed like they were winding through a deep forest. At others, he could make out where the trees came to an end, but what was on the other side? A grassy yard? A hidden cove?

They hadn't seen Amos for a while when a shrill bark cut through the woods. "It's him," Willa said. "He's up ahead."

As they grew nearer, they heard a rustling. It was the sound of a struggle. Willa took quick, short steps, dodging rocks and holes. The path had all but disappeared. They weren't on a proper trail anymore, but Amos had still found what they were looking for. Up ahead, Willa could make out the creamy color of Starbuck's coat.

Amos gave a bark of encouragement just as Willa and Ben ducked under a tree branch to reach them.

"Starbuck, you're caught," Willa said as she approached the startled pony. "Don't you worry. We'll get you out." She ran a hand along the mare's neck, and Starbuck let out a heavy sigh.

"It's a vine," Ben pointed out. "It's between her front legs." He tried to reach for it, but Starbuck pulled away. She shifted, straining against the prickly vine. Her eyes flashed with fear as she realized she was still trapped. Ben stepped back. "It's okay. You're okay."

"We'll figure it out," Willa promised, holding on to the pony's halter. "We'll figure it out," she repeated, but she had no idea how.

Chapter 10

NEITHER WILLA NOR BEN WANTED TO LEAVE Starbuck. Even though morning sunlight was now filtering through the trees, they couldn't see a clear path. They didn't know where they were. It seemed like Starbuck had gone to a lot of trouble to end up in the middle of nowhere.

"We should stick together," Willa said, still

gripping Starbuck's halter. Ben nodded. He now stood at Starbuck's side, using two fingers to rub her neck in tiny circles. The motion seemed to calm her, and it made him feel better too.

Willa was the one who had remembered that Ben had his walkie-talkie, and it came in very handy. Ben buzzed Chipper, who had his walkie-talkie right at his bedside, like a loyal best friend would. Chipper had his dad call Grandma Edna and Grandpa Reed right away.

So all Willa and Ben had to do was wait, and soothe Starbuck, and hope that this wasn't the last straw—the reason that Grandma Edna would insist she needed to find a new home for the pony.

Willa crossed her fingers for luck. She crossed

only one set because Lena had told her that two would cancel each other out. They couldn't have that. They needed all the help they could get. They needed to make sure Starbuck was not leaving Miller Farm.

The two siblings didn't dare talk about punishment, but Ben and Willa were both thinking about it. There had never been a rule against going outside in the tiny hours of the morning and trekking through the woods without telling anyone, but it was kind of obvious that kids shouldn't do that. They were pretty sure they'd get in trouble.

"Willa! Ben! Amos! Starbuck!"

Amos was the first to return Grandma Edna and Grandpa Reed's calls. He did so with three snappy barks.

"We're over here." Willa's call was much softer. She didn't want to startle Starbuck, who had finally settled down.

"Hold tight." Grandpa's voice was gruff and muffled.

"On our way!" Grandma's rang out like a dinner bell.

Ben held his breath as their grandparents appeared through the thick green of the late-summer plants. Their faces were flushed pink. Tiny beads of sweat glistened on their noses.

"Thank goodness," Grandma said when she got a good look at them. "Everyone okay? Anyone hurt?" She set her veterinarian kit on the damp ground and began to make her rounds. She glanced at Ben and offered a reassuring smile, and then she put her hands on either side of Willa's face and gave her a good stare.

"We're fine," Willa said, "but Starbuck is caught. We can't get her loose."

The vet moved her hand to the pony's neck and then down to her leg. "That's a girl," she murmured as she ducked under the mare's belly to figure out just how tangled the pony and the vine had become.

"Could've been a whole lot worse," she announced, straightening up. "Reed, I think this is a job for you and your pocketknife. Kids, you keep Starbuck calm. She needs to be absolutely still."

Grandpa Reed rummaged around and pulled out a knife with a maroon case and lots of slots for blades. Ben scowled when Grandpa unfolded one that was shaped like a small spear. It looked so sharp. Was it safe to use so close to Starbuck?

Grandpa got right to work. "Didn't think I'd be pruning vines at this hour," he said, all hunched over. His arm made short sawing motions. Willa concentrated on petting Starbuck's muzzle. The pony lowered her head, resting it on Willa's shoulder. Willa could feel the warmth of her, and hear the peaceful rhythm of her breath.

After a while Grandpa got down on his knees to go after the piece that was wrapped around Starbuck's hoof. "That just about does it," he announced a few minutes later, pushing himself up with a grunt. "Now, how do we get this pony home?"

"That's just what I was trying to figure out,"

Grandma Edna replied. "We've got ourselves a rare situation."

Willa felt her heart clench. She had been dreading this moment. She looked over at Ben. His eyes were pinched with worry. They couldn't listen, not if Grandma was going to send Starbuck away.

"It isn't safe to take the trail back to the farm. I'm not sure how that pony made it this far without getting hurt, not to mention the two of you in the dark." Willa and Ben forced themselves to meet their grandma's gaze. Her blue eyes could sometimes appear overly serious, but not now. Now they were soft and sincere.

"We're relieved everyone is all right," Grandpa mumbled in agreement.

"But I think we need to talk about Starbuck

getting loose. That's two times now. And we should probably ask ourselves why."

This is it, Willa thought. She bit her lip, preparing herself for bad news.

"I'm not so sure this pony was running away from home," Grandma Edna continued, "as much as she was running *to* one."

Willa and Ben looked at each other, confused.

Grandma Edna spoke again, deliberately. "I think Starbuck is trying to tell us something. I think she's ready for her new home." What was Grandma saying? It was like she was speaking in code. Willa dropped her gaze and studied her boots. They were caked in mud, like Ben's, and her bare feet were sweaty inside. She couldn't believe that they'd tracked Starbuck all the way here and Grandma still wanted to send her to another home.

"But we really love her," Ben said. "We think she's the greatest." Willa nodded in agreement.

"And she feels the same about you," Grandma Edna said.

Hearing this, Willa thought her heart would explode. Why was life so hard? She wrapped her arms around Starbuck's warm neck and let the tears stream down her cheeks.

When she heard a repeated clicking, she looked up. Ugh. Why was Grandma Edna typing on her phone at a time like this? Then she heard a door slam shut. That was odd. Willa had thought they were in the middle of nowhere.

"Willa? Ben?" That was Mom's voice. It was

faint, but Willa knew it was her mother.

"What's Mom doing all the way out here?" she asked Grandma.

Grandma's eyes danced when she smiled. "You kids don't know where we are, do you?"

They both shook their heads.

"You don't think Starbuck would go to all this trouble just to lead you to a dead end, do you?" Grandma joined Willa and Ben, right up close to Starbuck's head. "They underestimated you, girl. Didn't they? They haven't figured it out yet. When they do, they'll be mighty impressed." Starbuck twitched her ears toward Grandma Edna and gave a quick snort in response.

"So where are we?" Ben asked, looking around the thick brush.

"It's like I told you. Starbuck wasn't running away from home, but running to it. Look through those leaves. What do you see?"

Willa squinted where Grandma was pointing. It was hard to see anything against the rising sun.

"Just the sky," Ben answered. "And maybe something white."

"Yes, something white," Grandma agreed. "Let's go."

Grandpa had been busy clearing a path in that very direction. "Watch for those thorny bushes," he warned. "Someone really needs to clean out these overgrown weeds."

As they walked, Willa felt something pricking at her skin. Goose bumps. She gripped Starbuck's halter more tightly, and the pony followed close behind. Ben kept glancing back at them. The plants began to thin, and something came into view. It was a barn. It was red. It looked like any old red barn. But just past the barn was a tall white house, and in front of the house were Mom and Dad.

Willa felt her tears return. How could Starbuck have possibly known where they lived? She couldn't. It was as plain as that. But here they were.

When Willa realized that Mom and Dad were in their nicest pajamas, she realized that Misty Inn had guests. The visiting couple had come out on the porch. Willa was certain they were admiring Starbuck. The Chincoteague pony lifted her head high, looking noble and wise.

The family all met and there were hugs for everyone. Dad knelt down to give Amos a pet. Mom brushed the hair from Willa's face and smiled. Ben went back to rubbing Starbuck's neck. No one really said anything, and Willa still felt confused and a little afraid. She was grateful when Ben finally spoke up.

"Is this real?" he asked.

The adults all laughed. "Yes," Mom said. Dad's arm was wrapped around her. "It only seems fitting for Misty Inn to have its very own Chincoteague pony."

"Starbuck just insisted on hurrying things up," Grandma explained.

"And that troublemaker Fancy was all too willing to help," Grandpa added. "Those two were in cahoots from the start."

Willa and Ben shared expressions of disbelief. It seemed impossible.

Grandma tickled the whiskers on Starbuck's lip as she spoke. "It's true. Fancy had a history of opening gates at her old home, but I doubt she'll be opening any more. I think she made her point."

So the adults assumed that Starbuck had been plotting to come live at Misty Inn all along? And that Fancy, the expert lock picker, had been in on the plan? It sounded so far-fetched. Had the adults really convinced themselves it was true? They acted as if the kids should have known that Starbuck would soon live there, that Starbuck would soon be their own.

Willa knew her friends would never believe it. She told herself it didn't matter. Somehow, they were all safe. And they were home.

Standing with everyone in a circle in the driveway, Willa felt the warmth of being surrounded by family. She smiled at Ben and felt the comfort of being understood. She placed her hand on Starbuck's face and felt the happiness of belonging, because they all belonged to one another. They were meant to be together, even when it wasn't that easy.

Willa promised herself she would remember this moment. She recalled how Dad had said that in real life, nothing was perfect. Willa suspected that Dad was right, but, deep in her heart, she knew that this was pretty darn close.

Finding Luck

♥

To Elinor, and everyone
at Bridle Hill Farm

Chapter 1

"STARBUCK, STOP THAT!" WILLA GIGGLED. THE pony snuffled Willa's shoulder and nibbled at the ends of her walnut-colored hair. Willa reached around and scratched the pony's whiskered chin.

"She's hungry," Ben said. He snapped stems of the clover that grew along the driveway, just out of the buckskin pony's reach. He held out the bouquet, tickling Starbuck's lips.

"How could she be hungry?" Mom asked, not even looking up from the garden patch she was weeding. "You give her fresh-picked treats all day."

Starbuck stretched out her neck and tried to lip at the white flower, but Ben quickly pulled it away.

"Please don't feed her any of the herbs and plants we're growing for the restaurant," Mom said, shaking a seed packet. Soon the kids' dad would be opening a restaurant right there, on the main floor of their house. It was going to be part of the family's bed-and-breakfast, which was called Misty Inn. Of course, they'd had only two guests so far, but they had all worked hard getting the old house ready.

"Don't tease her," Willa insisted. She scowled at her brother.

"I don't want to spoil her," Ben claimed. A sly smile played at the corner of his mouth.

"Just give it to her, Ben," Mom said, "but then call it quits. If you keep hand-feeding her, she'll forget how to graze like a normal horse."

Willa knew that wasn't true. Starbuck was too smart to forget something like that. Besides, grazing came naturally to horses.

"Sometimes I forget she's here," Ben confessed, combing his fingers through her black mane. "And it's like a big present when I look in the field."

"Me too," Willa agreed. "But sometimes it feels like she's always been here. Doesn't it?" It was a funny thing for Willa to say. After all, the Dunlaps hadn't lived at Misty Inn that long. It had been less than a year ago that their family had moved to Chincoteague Island. The large Victorian house was very different than their tiny apartment in the big city of Chicago.

Starbuck had come to live at Misty Inn several months later, in the fall. The pony had spent almost the whole summer at their grandma's rescue center. While she was there, the kids had helped Starbuck get better from a leg injury. After that, they had worried that Grandma Edna would find a new home for the sweet mare. Their grandma was very practical with the animals at the rescue center. "Miller Farm is not a place for pets," she often said.

In the end, it was clear that Starbuck was the one who chose her new home—and she chose to be with the Dunlaps. It was also clear that Grandma Edna understood that they belonged together.

Now it was spring. "It doesn't matter how long she's been here; it just matters that she stays here," Ben said.

Starbuck whinnied and threw her head in the air. "Starbuck agrees," Willa said.

Ben laughed, and their puppy, Amos, barked. With his tail wagging, he circled Ben's feet. Amos was new to Misty Inn too. He had arrived with Buttercup, a neighbor's horse who lived in the old barn.

The only one who had real history at the house was New Cat. As a stray, the tabby cat had enjoyed her afternoons on the sunny, warm porch.

In fact, that was where she was resting now. New Cat was sprawled out, her green eyes barely open. Her ear twitched at the sound of a motor. She forced her lazy eyes open as the noise came closer.

"It's Grandma!" Ben called, waving toward an old, red pickup truck that pulled into the driveway.

"Afternoon, Dunlaps," Grandma Edna said. She reached to pick up a package from the other seat. "I've got something for you."

"For me?" Ben asked. Willa shook her head.

"For all of you," Grandma said. The skin around her eyes crinkled when she smiled. "But mostly for your parents, I guess."

Willa turned to see her mom's face. Were adults used to getting surprise packages?

Grandma Edna slid out of the truck and held out her freckled arms. The present was wrapped in brown paper, tied with twine.

"Hi, Mom." The kids' mom tucked the seed packet in the pocket of her gardening apron.

"Hello, dear," Grandma responded. "This is something to help you on your way."

Willa and Ben exchanged glances. Grandma Edna almost always said what was on her mind. But lately they had noticed that she was dropping hints. She didn't always say what she really meant. Willa wondered if she was doing that now.

Mom started to pull at the wrapping, but then Ben rushed forward and ripped the paper wide open. "What is it?" Ben asked.

"It's a banner," Grandma said. "It says 'Grand Opening.' It is for your bed-and-breakfast. You'll have a full house next weekend."

Mom gasped. "What?"

"My friend runs an inn on the far side of the island," Grandma explained. "She accidentally double-booked all her rooms, so I said you would take her extra guests."

"What?" Mom repeated.

"You really can't put off opening this inn any

longer, dear," Grandma Edna said. "You and Eric have to be in business by summer if you want to be a success."

"Did I hear Edna Miller out here?" Dad appeared on the porch, holding a whisk in his hand. He was smiling.

"My mom just found us a house full of guests for next weekend," Mom told Dad.

"An inn full of guests," Grandma Edna corrected. "You are about to officially open your bed-and-breakfast. It isn't just a house anymore. It's an inn."

Grandma returned to her truck and, before she drove away, called out the window, "I'm excited for you!"

Willa looked at Dad. The whisk now dangled at his side. His smile was gone.

Next Willa looked at Ben. He had been staring at Starbuck, but he glanced back at his sister. Willa could tell he was as worried as she was. If the two of them wanted to stay on Chincoteague and keep Starbuck, they would have to get to work.

Chapter 2

"THAT IS *VERY* SOON," DAD SAID. HE WAS LOOKING at the calendar on his phone. Dad walked over and sat down on the porch swing. "Seriously soon," he added.

"I can't believe my mother did this to us," Mom replied.

"If it's a grand opening, the restaurant has to be ready too," Dad realized out loud. He rubbed his chin. "I don't even have a produce supplier yet."

Willa knew what a produce supplier was. Dad had used one at his job back in Chicago. "Produce" was a word for fruits and vegetables. The "produce supplier" brought all the fresh food directly to the restaurant so Dad wouldn't have to go to the grocery store to shop for everything.

"And I'll have to tell Russo's I won't be able to work nights anymore." Dad had been filling in as a cook at an Italian restaurant. He wouldn't be able to work both places at once.

Ben stared at Willa. The whole reason their family had moved to Chincoteague Island was so Dad could open his own restaurant and Mom could run a bed-and-breakfast. At first,

Willa and Ben hadn't been sure it was a good idea. They had liked Chicago, and they had liked their friends there. But, after a while, Chincoteague had begun to feel like home. They had made wonderful new friends. Most of all, they now had Starbuck. If their parents' plans for Misty Inn didn't work out, it would mean another move for the Dunlaps. The kids understood that. They also knew that a different town would mean a lot more changes. Chances were that they wouldn't be able to take Starbuck with them. Neither Willa nor Ben could bear the thought of that.

Willa could feel the worry churning in her belly. She had to do something. "You're both being silly," she announced. "Grandma's right. It's time to get cracking."

Mom and Dad raised their eyebrows but didn't say a word.

Willa walked over to Mom, who was scowling at a long, narrow strip of paper that she had pulled out of her pocket. Willa gently pulled the paper from Mom's hand. It was a list. She skimmed it.

* order new mailbox
* plant rosebushes
* paint parking sign
* buy vases for dinner tables
* AND a lot of other things

"There isn't anything on here that *has* to be done before we open, is there?" Willa insisted, not waiting for either of her parents to answer.

"We don't need more to-do lists; we just need to do it."

Of course, Willa had never opened a bed-and-breakfast before. She didn't know exactly what was and wasn't needed. She just needed to convince her mom and dad that they were in good shape. She sure hoped they were, anyway.

Last fall the Dunlaps had all worked to get the bed-and-breakfast ready for its first visitors. In order to make it happen, Mom had stopped talking about all the things they had to do and had started making lists instead. Ever since the success of that trial weekend, Mom had kept making lists. She had made hundreds by now. She could always find more ways to improve Misty Inn.

It wasn't that Willa didn't like lists. She actually *loved* lists, even more than Mom. But she knew when enough was enough.

"And, Dad," Willa added, thinking fast, "sure, you'll need a produce guy. But think about all the stuff you already have." She took Dad by the hand. She led him into the kitchen and opened the pantry door. Ben followed right behind.

The pantry at Misty Inn was no ordinary pantry. Willa had seen pictures of the closets of famous actresses and singers, with shelves for shoes and color-coded hangers for fancy gowns. She thought of her dad's pantry as the same thing, but for chefs.

"Just look," Willa said. "You are totally set."

In one glance, Willa saw seven types of salt, four different kinds of paprika, and more than a half dozen brands of flour. Vanilla extract, vanilla beans still in the pods, and vanilla syrup. There were also dried versions of all the herbs Mom had planted in the flower beds, hanging in upside-down bouquets from the top shelf. "Dad, you're a chef. You love to make food. You should be excited to get started."

Ben reached out and pulled a stack of hand-written recipes off the shelf. He handed them to Dad. "Time to cook *your* recipes, Dad."

Their dad had always worked for a big restaurant, and another chef, often a famous one, had been in charge. The restaurant at Misty Inn was not big, but it was Dad's first chance to be the head chef. It was his first chance to make his own menu with all his own recipes, too.

"You know, kids, I think you're right," Dad admitted, smiling at Willa. He held the food-stained pages of recipes in one hand and pulled Ben close with the other. "Thanks, you two. Mom and I needed the pep talk."

"Just a little tighter," Mom called to Dad. "And to the left."

It was the next day, and Dad was up on the roof of their house. It seemed like he had been there for an hour. Willa and her friend Sarah Starling had ridden bikes, played five rounds of War with cards, and staged four tree-climbing races since he had first crawled out the upstairs window.

Dad was putting up the GRAND OPENING banner. Mom wanted it to hang between the two

windows on the third floor. Willa kept her eye on him as she played.

Dad inched his way toward the far side of the banner. His body was tilted forward and his feet were spread wide as he tried to keep his balance. A brisk wind was coming from the ocean. It whipped the banner right out of Dad's hands.

"You need to secure the bottom corners,"

Mom instructed. Willa caught her breath as Dad stumbled forward. The wind lifted his baseball cap off his head.

"Dad, come down!" Willa yelled. She ran over to where Mom watched.

"I've almost got it," he insisted, raising his voice.

"He'll be fine," Mom said, resting her hand on Willa's shoulder. "Your dad's very sure-footed."

Just then a rumble sounded. Willa looked up and spotted a black cloud. It seemed like it had appeared out of nowhere. It now hung directly over Assateague.

Assateague was the thin barrier island that lay between Chincoteague and the open sea. It was home to two herds of wild ponies.

From up where Dad was, he could probably see the old lighthouse on Assateague. The red-and-white lighthouse had been there for more than a hundred years and still shone a beam as a warning to ships at sea.

Another roll of thunder sounded like hooves pounding across the sky. The black cloud was crossing the bay.

"Dad, hurry!" Willa cried. Sarah had now joined her next to Mom.

Mom was glancing out toward the sea. "Yes, dear. Hurry! A storm is coming."

"Sarah! Sarah!" It was Ben, running from up the street. He had been at the Starling's. "You have to go home. Your parents told me to tell you they need help getting the animals in before it rains."

"But the horses and goats can stay out in the rain," Sarah said with a shrug.

"I don't think this is just any rain, Sarah," Mom said, looking at the dark clouds spreading across the sky. "You should head home now, sweetie."

A growl of thunder forced Sarah and Willa to say their good-byes. As soon as Sarah reached the end of the driveway, plump raindrops began to fall.

Chapter 3

IT DIDN'T TAKE MOM LONG TO CHECK THE weather forecast on her phone. When she did, she insisted Dad get down right away.

"Don't worry about the banner," Mom called. "We can open the inn without a banner. We can't open without *you*!"

As soon as she saw Dad crawl back through the window and give a thumbs-up sign—indicating

he had hung the banner in spite of the weather—
Mom put the rest of the family to work.

Willa and Ben's first job was to bring
Starbuck and Buttercup inside. The animals
would be safer—and drier—in their stalls
with flakes of hay to keep them busy. Of
course, Amos also needed his dinner since
he'd stay with the horses. Next the kids
rolled their bikes into the barn.

The few raindrops falling were heavy and
thunder kept booming. Slate-colored clouds
were above, bringing on an early night.

Mom hurried around, making sure all the old
house's shutters were latched closed. She turned
over the outside furniture. "Search the yard for
anything that could be lifted and carried by a
strong wind," she said, picking up a rake and a

short shovel. When she put her gardening tools in the barn, she grabbed a bungee cord.

"Help me with the grill!" Mom yelled to Willa, waving the cord over her head.

Willa hurried over to the patio, her arms wet with the rain. The wind crept into her cotton dress, making it balloon out in all directions. "You really think this thing is going any-where?" Willa asked, looking at the big black appliance with the propane tank underneath.

"Best to be on the safe side," Mom yelled over the swirling wind. She stretched the color-ful cord around the deck railing and then handed the other hooked end to Willa.

"I think it's better to be *inside*," Willa answered. She tugged on the cord until it was tightly secured around the barbecue.

"Yes," Mom agreed. "Let's go." She grabbed Willa's hand and they ran, their hair and clothes streaming behind them. They escaped inside through the kitchen door just as a clash of thunder cracked in the sky.

The rumbles of thunder and patter of rain were muffled in the big house. Willa immediately felt more at ease when Mom wrapped her in a towel. "I'm going to get dry clothes," she said with a shiver. She passed Ben on the stairs.

"It's movie weather!" Ben announced, his sleeping bag trailing behind him.

"I'll make popcorn," Dad offered. Willa saw Mom roll her eyes. Willa guessed her mom was still in high gear, wanting to do more to fix up the inn.

"Come on, Amelia," Dad said, his head in the pantry. "Mother Nature is telling us to take a break. I can make you a bowl without butter."

"Popcorn without butter?" Mom asked. "What's the point?" She smiled at Dad.

"Come help pick a movie," Ben called from the sofa. And that's when the lights flickered and went out.

"The TV died," Ben groaned. "No movie."

"What's Mother Nature telling us now?" Mom wondered out loud.

"Popcorn and board games by candle-light!" Willa said from the landing. She then rushed down the stairs and opened the game cabinet. She didn't want to miss out on family time. "That's exactly what Mother Nature's saying."

The Dunlaps played through the howling wind and pouring rain. The kids flinched when the crackles of the storm were fierce, but they huddled close. They played until Willa and Ben were too tired to climb the stairs for bed, so they slept—in sleeping bags—on the family-room floor. They knew they wouldn't be allowed to do anything like that when the inn was full of guests.

"Look at this," Mom grumbled as she opened the front door. It was the next morning, and the yard was a soggy patchwork of sticks and leaves. A thin layer of sand covered everything.

The kids checked on Starbuck and Buttercup first thing. When they opened up the barn, Starbuck whinnied a hello. Even though the pony didn't like to be cooped up, Willa knew they couldn't put her or Buttercup out in the field. The ground was still too wet.

Dad approached from the other side of the house. "I've got some bad news," he said. Willa and Ben followed their parents around to the back, the toes of their rain boots sinking in the marshy grass.

"Apparently those lightning flashes were closer than we thought." Dad pointed to a tree. It was an old black willow, its branches reaching higher than the house.

"It lost a limb," Ben whined.

"It broke a window," Dad added. He pointed toward the house. "In our *best* guest room."

"Do you think there's water damage?" Mom asked.

"There's only one way of knowing," Dad answered, looking up to the third floor. "When we moved to be by the water, I didn't plan on so much of the water actually being in our house." Last year they had had a plumbing problem that had flooded the whole top floor.

"That was just one other time," Mom insisted.

"One time, but weeks of cleanup." Dad bent down, starting to gather some of the sticks and small branches that littered the ground.

"I don't want to know what Mother Nature is telling us now," Ben grumbled.

"She's telling us to stop worrying about little things and just deal with the big stuff," Willa said in a bright, optimistic voice. Personally, Willa couldn't believe that they had to deal with another setback, but she didn't want her parents to feel discouraged.

"This is big all right," Dad agreed. "A big mess."

"I'll go and check on the room upstairs," Mom said. Her feet squished as she walked away.

"Ben and I can pick up the yard," Willa volunteered. "We are here to help!"

Dad sighed. "Thanks, but I should check for broken glass and other stuff first." He took another deep breath, checking out the damage. "But you're right, Willa. In the big scheme, things aren't that bad. How about you go look in on our neighbors? Start with Mrs. Cornett. Make sure she's okay."

"Good idea, Dad," Willa replied. "Mrs. Cornett's

chickens are wacky enough as is. I hope they weren't too scared during that storm."

"They were probably running around like chickens with their heads cut off!" Ben said, laughing so hard he could barely talk.

"Ben, that's gross," Willa scolded. "And not very funny."

"Maybe not to you," Ben said. "Or the chickens." He closed his lips tight, but giggles escaped out his nose.

"Good luck," Dad said, patting their backs, as they walked off toward their neighbor's house.

"You too!" Willa called.

Mrs. Cornett lived by herself. Her house was the next one down the road from Misty Inn. It wasn't far, but there was a cluster of trees in between so you couldn't see the little yellow cottage with lots of plants and flowers.

Willa hoped Dad's suggestion was a sign that they weren't that bad off, that they should take time to think of others. Of course, there was also the chance that Dad was just trying to get rid of them so he and Mom could sulk about the inn on their own.

Chapter 4

"I'M SO GLAD YOU KIDS CAME BY," MRS. CORNETT said. "That storm scared the eggs right out of my hens. I have more eggs than the Easter Bunny. I keep finding them all around the yard."

Mrs. Cornett must have been up for hours. She had already made several dozen of her famous deviled eggs, and she was starting to "whip up" something else. Tan, white, and pale-blue eggshells were piled by the cutting board.

"She seems fine," Willa whispered to Ben. They were in Mrs. Cornett's kitchen, which looked like a diner from an old movie, with a shiny metal counter and tall bar stools. "No trees fell on her house. Maybe we should go home and help there."

"Yeah," Ben answered. "Maybe."

"I tell you what, kiddos." Mrs. Cornett reached for a big metal bowl as she spoke. "You herd up my loose hens, and I'll make you some scrambled eggs. They'll be fluffy. I promise you that."

"It's a deal," Ben said, pushing himself off a stool.

"I don't think eating a second breakfast is

what Dad had in mind when he sent us over here," Willa said under her breath, hoping Mrs. Cornett wouldn't hear. Willa wondered how Mom and Dad were doing back at the inn.

"Chasing chickens sounds like fun. And you heard Mrs. Cornett," Ben said. "She needs help. We're doing her a favor."

"You kids sure are," the woman said. "I'm too old to chase those silly birds."

Just a few minutes later Willa and Ben were outside, panting.

"Try to get Hattie," Willa said, stopping to catch her breath. "She's the ringleader."

Hattie was a striking-looking chicken. Each of her bright white feathers had a black border, and her comb and wattle were cherry red against the yellow of her sharp beak. The kids knew it was sharp. Mrs. Cornett had the scars as proof. The hens were always escaping the coop. They often wandered over to the Dunlaps' yard, and Hattie was the hardest to convince to go home.

Ben tiptoed behind Hattie as she pecked in the strawberry patch. The chicken didn't seem to notice Ben. But as soon as he spread his

arms wide for the capture, she jutted off, clucking and flapping her wings. The other chickens scattered, and Ben collapsed in the grass . . . smack onto an egg!

"Yuck," Ben screeched. Raw egg dripped from his hand.

"You thought this would be fun?" Willa said, wiping sweat from her face. She leaned against the trunk of a fruit tree.

"I was wrong," Ben admitted.

As soon as the chickens were back in their coop, Mrs. Cornett asked the kids to pick bush beans and peas from her garden. It was nearly lunchtime before they were done. After their meal of scrambled eggs, she sent them off with a basket of what they had harvested, plus some ruby-red radishes.

As they walked home, Willa noticed that despite all the wind and weather, the GRAND OPEN-ING banner had remained in place. It didn't even look battered. The letters were bold and bright.

Still, Willa had a bad feeling. The more she thought about it, the more she believed Dad had been trying to get rid of them so he and Mom could deal with the inn on their own. They could never finish without help. As she and Ben walked past the front porch on the way to the kitchen door, she could hear her parents' raised voices through the open windows.

"But why are all the flashlights in the closet on the *first* floor?" Mom asked.

"It just makes sense to store them together," Dad insisted.

"But what if the lights go out and we're all

on the *third* floor?" Mom said. "That's where the guests will be."

Willa grabbed Ben's elbow before he reached the door. "We can't just walk in. They're arguing."

"The electricity is back on," Ben whispered, confused. "Who cares where the flashlights are?"

Willa shrugged. She guessed the quarrel wasn't *really* about flashlights.

But now it seemed like things had quieted down. She looked at Ben, and he raised his eyebrows. Just as she was about to turn the doorknob, she heard a door slam. "And where are all the batteries?" Mom yelled.

"In the toy bin under Ben's bed!" Dad called back.

"Why are they there?"

Willa and Ben sat down on the steps by the door. At least they had Mrs. Cornett's sugar snap peas to snack on while they waited for the argument to end.

From where they sat, Willa and Ben could see inside the open barn doors. They could just make out Starbuck's head as she nibbled from her hay net. They would both visit her later, but they had to have an important brother-sister discussion first.

They made a pact, a solemn promise, that they would do whatever they could to help Mom and Dad. They hated when their parents argued, even when it was about a silly thing like a flashlight—*especially* when it was about a silly thing like a flashlight!

They agreed they would take on whatever

jobs they could, and they would not let their parents tell them not to help. It was their house too! They would be ready for the inn's opening. It was Sunday, and the guests were coming on Friday.

All along, the plan had been to call the bed-and-breakfast Misty Inn and the restaurant the Family Farm. Willa had always liked the name of the restaurant. It sounded so cozy and welcoming. But at that moment, crouched on that narrow step, Willa didn't think the house felt cozy *or* welcoming. They had less than a week, but Willa was going to do her best to make that name fit!

Chapter 5

MOM AND DAD NODDED AND SMILED AS THE KIDS presented their plan at dinner that night. Their parents admitted things had been hectic. "We promise to give you a list of ways you can help," Mom said. "But there are just some chores kids can't do."

"Or parents," Dad added. "Most parents can't replace a one-hundred-year-old window.

We were lucky we found a carpenter who can do it this week."

"You can have my room," Ben offered out of nowhere, his cheeks turning pink. "For the inn, if you need it. I'll clean it and everything." He hadn't even touched the sausage meatballs on his pasta. They were his favorite.

Willa watched as Mom and Dad looked at each other. She wondered what they were thinking. "That's very sweet, Ben," Mom said. "But we'll be fine. It'll all get done, and you can stay in your own room. This may soon be an inn, but it will always be your home, too." Mom's eyes were warm and kind when she looked at Ben, but her expression changed as she glanced down at her plate.

"I just remembered!" Willa yelled out. "It's a teacher prep day on Friday, so we don't have school. We can help right up to the moment the guests come!" Willa felt so relieved. She and Ben could really make a difference then.

Mom and Dad didn't look so sure. "We'll see," Dad said. "Maybe all the work will already be done."

"Maybe," Willa said, trying to sound as reassuring as possible, but she could tell her parents were worried, which made *her* worry too. After giving Dad a hand putting the dishes in the dishwasher, Willa sneaked out to the barn.

Starbuck and Buttercup were still in their stalls. Clouds had lingered in the sky all day, so the sun had not had a chance to dry the pasture. Willa first offered Buttercup a treat of carrot tops before heading over to spend time with Starbuck.

Starbuck nickered, stretching her neck for her own treat. The pony eagerly ate the green stems and rested her head over Willa's shoulder. "Sorry, no actual carrots today," Willa told Starbuck. "Dad's saving up for the restaurant recipes." Starbuck didn't seem to feel cheated. She seemed content. It comforted Willa, hearing the even munching of the pony's jaw, her easy breath.

Tomorrow was Monday. Willa had hardly thought about school, other than how no school on Friday would give her and Ben time to help. At the beginning of the school year, she and Ben had always been busy. They had wanted to try to finish their chores at home so they could hurry to Grandma Edna and Grandpa Reed's farm to see Starbuck. Once the pony had come to live at Misty Inn in the fall, they had not had to rush around all the time.

"I hope we'll have time for a ride this week," Willa murmured. Starbuck sighed. It seemed to Willa that the pony understood how important the opening of the inn would be. Willa wrapped her arms around the pony's neck. "I hope so," she said again.

♥

Willa and Ben were true to their word. They did extra chores every evening to get the inn closer to being ready. Because she had nice handwriting, Mom had Willa make a sign for the check-in table and place cards for all the guests at dinner. Just to get the hang of it, she practiced by making a card for both herself and Ben. Ben's job was to roll the fancy silverware in the cloth napkins for dinner.

"Why are we doing this little stuff when there's still a hole in a bedroom window upstairs?" Ben wondered as he lined up the napkin corners.

"Because we do what we can," Willa said, admiring the new dining-room setup. There were now five wooden tables for guests to use while enjoying breakfast or dinner. The tables didn't match, yet each had its own charm. It was starting to look like a real inn! But each day there were also little setbacks.

The carpenter had come to install the guest-bedroom window on Wednesday. The replacement looked as good as new, but the carpenter tripped on the porch steps on his way out. His foot went straight through a rotten board. "I'm all booked tomorrow," he said. "But I can come back to fix it Friday morning."

Willa and Ben passed the carpenter in the driveway as they got off the bus. After the man drove off, Dad collapsed on the front lawn. "As soon as he replaces the board, we have to paint it, and the paint has to dry before anyone can use the stairs." He paused, his baseball hat pulled over his eyes. "Even if he shows up first thing Friday, that's cutting it close."

Mom bent down to pat Dad on the shoulder, but she only comforted him for a minute. "Okay, kids," she then announced. "Out of your school clothes. You have a manure pile to move."

"Do we *really* have to move the manure?" Ben asked moments later, holding his nose with one hand and a pitchfork in the other.

"You can unplug your nose," Willa said. "It's so old it doesn't smell that bad anymore." Willa knew what he meant—the job didn't seem super important. Still, Willa was going to move every chip of manure from where they'd stacked it for months on the side of the field to the spot behind the barn, right where Mom had pointed.

Even if it wasn't an important job, it was a

big one. The wheelbarrow tipped over . . . twice. Ben lost his footing and ended up sitting in the stuff. *Gross!* And even though she thought she was careful, Willa had two boots full of dry horse poop before they were done.

"Why do we have to eat out here with the bugs?" Ben groaned when the family took a dinner break.

"It keeps the crumbs outside," Mom had explained. "And the kitchen clean. Unlike you." Ben half smiled, his teeth a bright white against his now-dirty skin.

Many blisters and drinks from the hose later, the brother-and-sister shoveling team was done. "I love Starbuck," Ben said, putting the pitchfork back in the barn, "but I wish she could use a toilet."

"We should clean up in the downstairs bath-room," Willa said as they headed inside, "so we don't track all over the house."

They left their filthy boots outside and then crammed inside the little bathroom, elbows and feet barely fitting. "Use soap," Willa reminded Ben. He picked up the bar and started to make suds. They watched as the bubbly water, brown with dirt, dripped from their hands.

They were almost finished when they heard footsteps. "Willa? Ben?" The door was flung open. "What are you doing in there?" Mom looked as if she had caught them in a trash dump.

"We're washing up so we don't make a mess upstairs," Willa said, proud that she had thought ahead.

Mom looked like she was about to cry. "This

was the one bathroom that I *had* cleaned."

Willa looked around and realized that the bar of soap had been new, and the towel, now crumpled in Ben's hands, had a fancy lace border on the bottom. *Oops!*

"Grandma wants to talk to you," Mom said, and she placed her cell phone in Willa's hand.

As Willa left the bathroom, she noticed a note pasted to the outside of the door.

CLEAN! DO NOT USE!

Thanks,

Mom

Chapter 6

"I REALLY DON'T KNOW, GRANDMA," WILLA SAID.
"Ben and I wanted to stay home and help with
the opening. Can we tell you tomorrow?" Ben
tried to push in closer. "Okay, bye."

"What'd she say?" Ben asked. He'd been
standing by her shoulder, his ear tilted toward
the phone.

"She wants to know if we want to go to

Assateague on Friday," Willa answered. "She's doing a special vet check on the wild ponies."

"Friday?" Ben asked. Willa nodded. Even though it was just a boat ride away, the Dunlap kids had not visited Assateague yet. To them, the tiny island that was the remote home of the famous Chincoteague ponies was still a mystery. Ever since Starbuck had come to live with them, they both felt like they had their own piece of the Assateague legend right there in their old red barn.

"What's on Friday?" Mom asked, striding into the kitchen, her arms full of candlesticks.

"The opening of the inn," Willa replied innocently.

"No," Mom said, shaking her head. "Something to do with Grandma."

Willa reluctantly told Mom about Grandma Edna's invitation.

"Well, you have to go!" Mom said. "It's such a good opportunity."

"But we want to stay here and help you and Dad," Willa said.

"Yeah," Ben chimed in.

"I think your dad will agree with me," Mom said.

Willa suspected that Mom wanted them to go, but not just because it was a good opportunity. She glanced hopefully at the clock. "Well, it's nearly bedtime," Willa said all of a sudden, raising her hands in an exaggerated shrug. "And it's a family rule that we can't make big decisions after eight o'clock. I guess it'll have to wait for tomorrow."

Mom rolled her eyes.

Willa had always thought it was a silly rule, but she was thankful for it now.

The next morning on the school bus, Sarah begged Willa to go on the trip. "You have to," Sarah said, grasping Willa's hand. "Dad is taking me and Chipper. Kids hardly ever get to go to the roundups on the island. It'd be so much fun to be there together."

Grandma had explained the details to Willa on the phone. The volunteer fire department of Chincoteague helped take care of the ponies. Three times a year a group of volunteers and local veterinarians gathered the wild ponies for checkups. The roundup in the middle of the summer included the great pony swim, when all the horses and ponies of the southern herd swam across the bay to Chincoteague.

The spring roundup was not as complicated. While the events of the pony swim took the entire weekend, this spring roundup would be done in a day. All the ponies would stay on Assateague.

"We can take our walkie-talkies," Chipper said to Ben. The idea made Ben smile. Now that he knew Chipper would be there, he wanted to go more than ever. He glanced at Willa. He could tell she hadn't decided.

"I'm not sure," Willa tried to explain. "My parents never hired a server for the inn, and Dad might need to run some last-minute errands. They might need me."

"You need a waitress?" Chipper asked, over-hearing the girls' conversation. "Katherine keeps telling Mom she needs a job. She wants to buy a car." Katherine was the oldest of the Starling kids.

"Is that true?" Willa asked Sarah.

"Well, yeah," Sarah replied. "She does."

"That's huge!" she exclaimed. "I'll bet Mom would hire her in a second." With that good news, Willa felt like things would come together. She felt like she and Ben could enjoy a trip to Assateague with Grandma and their friends. She convinced herself that Mom and Dad could take care of the last-minute details by themselves. They were grown-ups, after all.

"Katherine? That's great," Mom said. "I'll call the Starlings right away."

Willa had finally found Mom in Ben's bedroom, ironing pillowcases.

"So, Ben and I decided to go to Assateague with Grandma tomorrow," Willa announced.

"Oh?" Mom replied. It was not the reaction Willa expected.

"Sarah and Chipper will be there," Willa explained. "And I double-checked with Grandma that we'll be back by evening. I can even probably help with dishes."

"Well, I don't think you'll need to do that," Mom said with a slight smile. She set the iron down and took a sheet of paper from her pocket. A list. She made a tiny clucking sound as she reviewed it. "Sweetheart," she began again, looking up at Willa. "I know you've been busy, but there are Popsicle sticks in the craft bin. Would you make markers for all the herbs?"

Willa couldn't tell if Mom was giving her silly

little jobs just to keep her busy. "But, Mom, I want to really help."

"That will be help," Mom answered.

As she headed down the stairs, Willa passed Dad on his way up. "Your brother needs a brush so he can make a 'Wet Paint' sign for tomorrow," Dad said. "Can you get him one? He's in the barn."

"Of course," Willa said.

"And keep an eye on the corn bread in the oven?" he called out from the second floor.

"Yes," Willa replied, making a list in her head.

First she located a paintbrush in the cupboard under the stairs. She ran it out to Ben, who was looking for leftover wood for the sign. When she came back to the house, she headed straight for the craft bin so she could make the markers for the garden. Then the doorbell rang. It was Katherine Starling, already there to ask about the job.

Willa called to Mom and heard a scratching at the back door. "New Cat? How did you get out?" Willa wondered as the cat strutted into the kitchen.

That's when Dad raced down the stairs. "Did you take out the corn bread?" he asked.

"Not yet," Willa said, looking at the clock. "The buzzer didn't go off."

"I didn't set one," Dad said. "I told you to keep an eye on it."

Willa had been busy doing other things! Didn't he get that?

Dad pulled the corn bread out. She could

see that the edges were tinged brown, darker and drier than Dad liked. It wouldn't be good enough for opening day.

"Don't worry, honey," Dad said. "I can make another batch tomorrow. It's always tastier fresh from the oven anyway." Dad placed the pan on the counter and pulled off the oven mitt. "Oh, I almost forgot, can you go find your mother? She wants you to show Katherine where we store some of the stuff around here."

All of a sudden, things felt very busy. Willa wondered whether she should stay home the next day. But the more she thought about it, the more she didn't want to. . . .

Chapter 7

"RISE AND SHINE. IT'S A BIG DAY."

Mom gave Willa's shoulder a shake before opening her bedroom curtains.

"It's a big day for you, too," Willa replied, squinting as light filled her room.

"You've got that right," Mom said. "Can you wake your brother?" Mom asked. "Grandma needs you two ready soon."

Willa's feet dragged as she made her way to Ben's room.

"Wake up, you," she said, throwing a stuffed hippo at Ben's head. "We're going to Assateague, and Mom and Dad are going to open an inn."

Ben sat straight up. "So I'm not battling a nest of dragons in the underworld?" he mumbled.

"Definitely not," replied Willa. "You need to stop playing video games right before bed."

"That's the only time I'm allowed to play them." Ben sulked.

"Get dressed," Willa said. "And close your door. You don't want any guests seeing this mess. Why aren't those clothes in the laundry bin?"

"Because they aren't dirty," Ben answered.

"You wore them to move the manure pile. Remember?" Willa told him, and stomped out of the room.

Even though they didn't agree on how dirty his clothes might be, Willa and Ben did agree that they needed to be home to assist Mom and Dad that night. As Willa was grabbing granola bars for their breakfast, she noticed a stack of long, thin papers next to the sink. *More lists*, she thought.

Willa was still thinking about all those lists nearly a half hour later as they climbed out of Grandma's car. Grandma led them down a sandy path where the trees arched overhead. The path ended in a hidden cove with one dock. At the dock was one small boat. They all climbed in.

"You ready?" Grandma called out as the

engine sputtered. Willa and Ben nodded and smiled, and Grandma guided the boat away from the dock using the handle on the motor.

Soon they had left the cove and entered the open water. Willa thought it was funny how normally this trip would have filled her every thought. She was crossing the bay, about to see the wild ponies of Assateague up close. Many visitors came to Chincoteague and only caught glimpses of the ponies as they escaped from the beach into the shadows of the trees. Willa knew how lucky she and Ben were.

She also thought of their Chincoteague pony back at Misty Inn. Before she had left that morning, with a chill still in the air, Willa had made sure to do her barn chores. She had thrown flakes of hay to Starbuck and Buttercup. She had made sure the large metal trough was full of water. The ponies on Assateague didn't have someone looking out for them every day. It was up to the herd to find grass for grazing and fresh water to drink.

As they sped across the bay in the cool gray of the cloudy morning, it seemed like most of the world was still asleep, except for an egret soaring in the sky. Things were very different once they arrived on Assateague.

As soon as they tied the boat to a dock, Willa could hear the whinnies.

"The cowboys should be just about done with the roundup by now," Grandma said. She lifted her vet kit from the floor of the boat. "They began near dawn, so they'll be good and ready for us."

Grandma was referring to the volunteers who helped with the roundups. The full term was "saltwater cowboys," because the cowboys and their horses often had to get in the water during the summer roundups. Sometimes, when the herd swam across the bay, there would be stragglers. It was up to the cowboys to keep the herd together.

Looking across the bay, Willa thought that Chincoteague looked far away.

"It's a shame you two haven't been to Assateague yet," Grandma said as they hiked through the sand. "I'm glad you came with me. Your folks are worried that you've been working too hard, doing too much work on the inn. I have to agree."

Willa and Ben looked at each other. Grandma

had a hard time keeping her opinions to herself. But this opinion surprised Willa. Grandma always said that kids should pull their own weight. Willa still worried that she hadn't done enough.

"Hey, look what I found!" Ben said, sifting through a clump of sea grass. "A coin! And it's old." Grandma and Willa leaned over and inspected the discovery.

Ben rubbed his finger over the silver-colored coin, brushing dirt and sand from its face. "Maybe it's from the Spanish shipwreck," Willa said. "The same one that brought the ponies to Assateague Island." Willa knew that Assateague wasn't where the cargo ship had been headed. A horrible storm had sunk the ship, but the ponies had managed to escape and swim to shore.

"See what wonders the world has to offer," Grandma murmured, on her way again. "Legend has it that you can make a wish on a coin collected from a shipwreck."

"A wish?" Ben repeated. It wasn't like Grandma to believe such things.

"A wish," she confirmed.

"Arrived on island," Ben stated in a short clip. "Found ancient coin."

Willa looked over her shoulder and realized Ben was speaking into his walkie-talkie. There was static followed by a jumble of words. Willa guessed that was Chipper responding.

"There's one of the paddocks," Grandma said, motioning ahead.

When she looked up, Willa could see Sarah with a small group by a tall white fence.

Sarah rushed forward, half running and half skipping. "Willa! You have to see this!" Sarah pulled her so close that Willa nearly bumped into her friend's extra-long, extra-high pony-tail as she ran behind her. They came to an abrupt stop at the paddock fence. "Isn't that foal the cutest!"

Sarah was right. With its deep brown eyes and wispy mane, its knobby white knees and sloppy splashes of chocolate brown on its neck and back, the foal was the cutest. It also looked like the loneliest. "Where's its mother?" Willa asked.

"The cowboys are trying to find her," Sarah answered. "She's not in this paddock or else she'd be with the foal, right?"

"Sure," Willa said, nodding. She put her elbows on the top rail of the fence and searched the paddock. It made sense that the mother would be with such a young foal. So if the mare wasn't in the fenced-in area, where could she be?

Chapter 8

"WHAT DO YOU THINK, EDNA?"

Mr. Starling and Grandma Edna were talking. All the kids were listening in. They were worried about the tiny foal, standing alone. Grandma had gone into the paddock to take a look. Now Mr. Starling wanted to hear Grandma Edna's opinion.

"I don't think they've been separated long,"

Grandma said. "The foal seems healthy and not too hungry, but he won't stay that way. He'll need milk soon."

Willa looked at the sweet foal. His eyelids drooped and then sprang open as he fought sleep.

"Someone's got to locate that mare," Mr. Starling said. "And fast." He looked at his son and daughter. He then turned to Ben and Willa. "Don't suppose you kids could help?"

"Yes, Daddy, please," Sarah begged.

"We can do it," Chipper agreed, and he handed his walkie-talkie to his dad. "Just call Ben if you need us."

Ben touched his own walkie-talkie, which was hanging from his belt. Willa realized that her brother had been quiet since the discovery of the little colt.

"I'm happy to give you all a job and get you away from the yard," Mr. Starling said, "but you can't go on your own. It's not safe."

With two other vets at the roundup, Grandma volunteered to go with them on the search for the mare.

"What'll happen if we can't find her?" Ben wondered out loud as the group marched off toward the trees.

"Well"—Grandma hesitated—"that little guy is young and still needs his mom's milk. He'll get thirsty and weak without it." Grandma walked at the lead, the kids jogging to match her pace. "But let's hope it doesn't get to that."

They first took a couple of loops around the area where the horses were corralled. Grandma thought the mare might be nearby. When they didn't see her, they headed deeper into the woods. Grandma planned to go back to where the cowboys had first spotted the herd that morning.

The island was a big place. The beach stretched for miles. There were docks and roads for tourists. Willa knew that the north side even had campgrounds, but there was also a lot of natural space. Tall pine trees shaded and sheltered the herds from the weather.

"How are we going to find a single pony?" Sarah asked after they had been hiking around for more than an hour. "She could be anywhere, especially if she darted off when the cowboys came through." Sarah said what the entire group was thinking.

"I don't know," Grandma admitted, "but the bugs have already found me."

The bugs had found everyone, and everyone was waving and swatting their hands. It made it hard to stay focused.

"What about the lighthouse?" Willa suggested. "Maybe we'll get a better view from there."

"Top-notch thinking," Grandma said. "Anyone have a compass?"

"I do," Chipper said. No wonder Chipper and her brother had quickly become such good friends. They both loved gadgets. Grandma checked Chipper's compass, changed direction, and kept swatting bugs.

They all stepped from the trees into the full light of the midday sun. They had snacked on their hike, and now they all stopped to drink water.

"It's just over there," Willa yelled, pointing to the tall red-and-white-striped brick tower. In front was a small building that looked like a one-room schoolhouse. Willa took off. Sarah ran close behind her, and the boys followed. Grandma continued at her well-paced walk.

When the girls arrived, they bolted up the two short steps to the house. Willa fumbled at the doorknob and found it was locked.

"No!" she moaned, pulling at the door.

"I thought it was *always* open," said Sarah.

Ben kicked at the sandy path.

"Did you try knocking?" Grandma asked.

At once, all four kids knocked. They were still knocking when the door swung open.

"Yes?" It was a park ranger, wearing a dark-brown hat, a tan shirt with badges, and sturdy boots.

"Please, sir, you have to let us in. We have to find a pony," Willa said.

"I don't think there are any ponies in here," the ranger replied, smiling to himself.

"No," Ben continued. "We need to use the lighthouse as a lookout. The pony is lost somewhere on the island, and her foal needs her."

The ranger's expression quickly changed. "I see," he said. "We're usually not open right now, but it sounds like an emergency." He stepped aside and motioned to the stairs.

It was a spiral staircase.

"You guys know it's haunted, right?" Chipper said, staring up.

"That's not true," Sarah said. "Even if it were, we have no choice."

"I'll wait for you here," Grandma said.

With that, Willa started climbing. The red metal steps seemed to go on forever. When she looked down, she felt dizzy. The clanging of four sets of feet rang in her ears. But she kept going. This was their best chance to find the mare. She thought of the hot sun and how thirsty the foal must be by now.

It was 175 feet straight up, and luckily the door to the metal deck was open.

"Be careful," Willa warned, holding Ben back from the railing.

The four friends looked out at the island. In places it was wooded; in others, pure sandy beach; and still others were filled with large patches of marsh grass, sprouting from the water like giant lily pads.

Willa noticed Ben take the coin out of his pocket. She realized he hadn't even shared it with Chipper. Her brother rubbed his fingers over the carved face. She wondered if he was making a wish.

"I think I can see your house!" Sarah announced. She had binoculars that the ranger had loaned to her.

"Really?" Willa asked.

"Yeah," responded Sarah. "I can see the 'Grand Opening' banner."

Willa had not thought about the inn for hours. Now she pictured her parents rushing around, Mom tending to last-minute details, Dad probably chopping vegetables.

"Where would she be?" Chipper asked under his breath.

Willa tried to answer Chipper's question. But it only made her think of questions of her own. Why would the mare not be with her foal? What could have happened? Was she okay?

Chapter 9

"WE FOUND HER! WE FOUND HER!"

Then came a frantic race down the winding staircase.

"It was Ben!" Sarah said when she reached the bottom. "Ben saw her first," Sarah explained to Grandma.

"She's not moving!" Chipper said, leaping down from the third step.

Willa and Ben were right behind the Starling kids.

Grandma quickly thanked the ranger. As they left, the kids tried to give her all the facts: The mare was not far, she seemed to be awake, and she was up to her knees in some mucky water.

"Mucky water?" Grandma said, thinking it through. "Sounds like she might be stuck. The wet sand can get slippery around here."

"Like quicksand?" Ben asked.

"Yes, in some ways," Grandma said.

Willa gulped. Quicksand did not sound good.

"Now, when we get there, I need you all to stay calm," Grandma advised. "She might very well be frightened, and you need to help her feel safe. So you stay safe too."

♥

"She doesn't seem scared at all," Sarah observed.

The mare did not seem alarmed. Her breath was steady. Her head hung low. She didn't even try to move away when the group approached. She stood still as the salt water rippled around her legs.

"Stay where the grass is thick," Grandma softly said, handing Willa a halter. "So you know you have solid ground. Nice and easy."

The pony barely blinked an eye as Willa latched the halter behind her ears. Her coloring nearly matched that of her foal.

Next Willa, still on a patch of sturdy marsh grass, attached a lead and clicked with her tongue. She tugged on the lead.

"That's right," Grandma encouraged. "Try to get her to get out of it."

The pony stretched out her neck, but she wouldn't take a step. Willa tugged harder. "Come on," she pleaded. The mare laid back her ears and strained against the halter.

"I don't think this pony is wild," Chipper said. "I think she's lazy."

"I wouldn't say that," Grandma replied.

"She's probably worn out," Ben stated. "I'll bet she tried to get loose before, and she's tired now."

"That's a good guess. So she needs a reason to move," Grandma declared. "The tide will come in soon."

Willa knew what that meant.

The water would get deeper, and it would be even harder to get the mare out!

It was nearly an hour later, and the girls had come up with a plan.

"It has to work," Willa said as she watched Mr. Starling approach. "It just has to."

In his outstretched arms, Mr. Starling carried the foal. It was slow going, as the pony was heavy. He sloshed through ankle-deep pools, headed straight for the group.

The mare had not tried to move since they had first arrived. The water had risen over her knees. While they had waited, they had poured fresh water into their hands so she could drink. Even though she was surrounded by it, the sea-water was too salty to quench her thirst.

She seemed even more tired than before, but her ears pricked forward when the stranger came close with her foal in his arms. She lifted her head and nickered a friendly greeting.

The foal returned the call, his nostrils flaring.

Willa clicked her tongue once again, hoping the paint pony would try to get herself unstuck.

"Right here, Dad," Sarah directed. The kids had decided where the foal would be safest. He needed to be away from the water, but he also needed to be close to his mother.

Mr. Starling lowered the foal onto its four

wobbly legs and then backed away. Sarah and Chipper joined him, next to Grandma.

Ben got down on his knees and wrapped his arm around the foal. "I know you want to be with her, but you can't go in the water," he said.

Willa stayed with the mare, loosely holding on to the lead. The pony stretched out her neck, but the foal was too far away. The foal reached out its neck as well.

"Come on, girl," Ben said.

The foal whinnied again, the pitch higher. The mare seemed content to stay where she was.

"What if we took him away?" Willa asked. She thought about how hard it would be to have something you love, and then deal with the idea of not having it. "She might try harder if she thought we were leaving with him."

"Nothing else is working," Grandma said, sounding discouraged.

"I think it's worth a shot," Mr. Starling said.

As soon as Mr. Starling lifted the young colt, it started calling out. Mr. Starling turned and took several steps away.

The foal's mother raised her head and whinnied, shrill and long. Fear flashed white in her eyes. "Come on," Willa said, putting pressure on the lead. The mare whinnied louder. Then Willa could see the pony's muscles tighten. Her hindquarters rounded as she strained. Her whole body seemed to pitch forward, and one of her back legs escaped the water with a splash.

"That's it, that's it," Willa said as one front leg surged out of the muck. "Keep coming." The next steps came easier, and soon the pony climbed onto the grassy ground next to Willa. She stumbled, pulling her way to her foal.

Mr. Starling moved quickly. As soon as the foal was back on his own feet, the weary colt walked to his mother. They touched noses, and the foal rested briefly under the shelter of his mother's neck, then ducked under her belly to drink milk.

"Well, that was lucky," Grandma said. "Wasn't it?"

"Lucky indeed," Mr. Starling agreed. His cheeks ballooned with air as he slowly exhaled.

"That should be his name," Sarah said. "Lucky."

Willa liked it. She thought it suited the sweet foal.

But she knew luck had had nothing to do with it.

Chapter 10

LUCKY AND HIS MOM WERE REUNITED. THE TINY foal flicked his fluffy tail as he trotted around the mare. Then he approached the four kids, eagerly sniffing their hands. "He's so friendly now," Chipper said.

"It's because she's here. Now he feels safe and can explore," Sarah explained to her brother.

Before long, Grandma told everyone they needed to head back to the roundup site.

"Can't we just leave them here?" Ben asked Grandma quietly. "She looks so tired. And Willa and I have to go home soon."

Willa had been thinking the same thing. The low sun was casting long shadows, which meant the afternoon was nearly over.

"It has been a long day for them, but they need to go back," Grandma said. "It's safer for them to be with the herd. And we need to make sure Lucky and his mom don't get stuck again, *especially* since they're so tired."

Willa led the mare, keeping close to Grandma and Mr. Starling, who took turns carrying the foal. Back at the paddock, Grandma and one of the other vets examined the young colt and his mother. They needed to confirm they were both okay. It had been a difficult day.

Once the checkup was over, Grandma took the halter off the mare. The wild pony immediately gave her head a good shake, her mane flopping from side to side.

"I'm satisfied. She seems good," Grandma said, closing the gate. She then turned to the kids, who had been anxiously waiting. "You all should be proud of yourselves. You did fine work."

Only now did the Starlings and Dunlaps realize they were shivering. The late-day sun had not dried their clothes. Their shoes were like sponges, but they had not noticed until now.

In the boat on the way home, Willa felt the worry of the day. Even with the sea air streaming past her face, her head and shoulders were still heavy.

Willa and Ben shared a silent glance. She knew they were both thinking of their parents and the inn. They had wanted to be home by now. They had wanted to be there before the guests arrived. But the sun was setting. The sky looked like different-colored jewels. The inn was probably already full.

"Funny," Grandma said, talking over the motor. "I was taking you two to Assateague so you could get a break from all the work. But you found an ever bigger project."

Willa just hoped Mom and Dad had not run into even bigger projects at home, too.

There were few words during the car ride home. Willa felt anxious as they neared the house.

"Thanks again," Grandma said. She stopped in front because the driveway was full of cars. "Want me to come in?"

"No," Willa answered quickly, already stepping from the truck. "We'll be fine. Thanks."

"Yeah," Ben said. "Thanks, Grandma."

"You're welcome," she said. "The place looks great."

Willa stood looking at the inn from the street. All three floors were glowing. A warm golden light shone from the windows. It looked pretty and peaceful from the outside, but Willa wondered what it was like inside.

Willa put a hand on Ben's shoulder, and they started walking up the driveway. They heard a door slam and were surprised to see Mrs. Cornett hurrying out the kitchen door.

"Well, hello, kiddos," she said, tucking a straw basket under her arm. "Just making a drop off for tomorrow morning. Congratulations on the inn."

"Thanks," Willa murmured, and she quickened her pace. When they passed the front porch, they saw Ben's handmade sign strung across the just-fixed front steps. WET PAINT.

Willa squeezed Ben's shoulder.

As they neared the kitchen door, Willa saw something move in the shadows.

"Hi, guys!" It was Katherine Starling, Sarah and Chipper's sister, who was helping in the kitchen. "Welcome back. Your dad just sent me out to cut some herbs."

"Do you need help?" Willa asked.

"Nope, I'm all set," she said. "They were all marked and everything."

Willa blushed, realizing she had marked the herbs. Ben stepped up and opened the door. Willa gave him a hopeful smile as they followed Katherine inside.

"Willa! Ben! I'll be right back," Mom called as she rushed into the dining area, a full plate in each hand.

"Mom looks nice," Ben whispered to Willa. Willa thought that Mom looked like Mom, but without the paint-splotched sweatshirt and wad of marked-up lists stuffed in her pocket.

"Hi, kids," Dad said, hugging them both from behind with his oven mitts on. "Are you hungry?" Dad's face was smudged, but his smile was bright.

"We saw Mrs. Cornett," Willa said, still confused by all the activity. "What was she doing here?"

"Oh! She's my produce supplier," Dad exclaimed. "At least for now. After you brought back her eggs and radishes and peas, I called her. She used to run a farm, and she has more veggies than she can eat."

"Isn't that great?" Mom had returned and chimed into the conversation. "And Katherine's amazing. Thanks for thinking of her, you guys."

"Sure thing," Ben said, snatching a cube of bread from a baking sheet on the counter. "Yum," he said, and grabbed another.

"Corn-bread croutons," Dad said. "I made them from that batch that overcooked yesterday. It was a good idea, if I do say so myself."

Willa took a bite. Buttery and crunchy. Pretty good for a burnt batch!

"You two must be starved." Mom tucked

a strand of hair behind Willa's ear. "Where do you want to eat? Here, in the kitchen. Or in the main dining room, so you can see Misty Inn all up and running?"

Willa looked toward the hallway that led to the dining room. It was lit with the same warm glow she had seen from outside. "I don't know, Mom. We're pretty dirty," she said, looking at her damp shoes.

"Don't be silly," Mom answered, wrapping Willa in a one-armed hug. "We are a family-run inn, and our restaurant is the Family Farm. I think it's okay that you're a little dirty." She lifted two plates from a stack and two sets of silverware, rolled up in a napkin. "Wash your hands and meet me at the table."

"I'll send you the best dish, for my two

best customers." Dad waved at them with his spatula and turned back to the stove top, which was full—full of pans that were sizzling, boiling, and simmering with good smells.

Willa and Ben sat down at a small table by a window. There was a view of the field. The night was clear and warm, and Starbuck and Buttercup were out. They looked at home.

"I hope Lucky and his mom are okay," Ben said. He placed something on the table. It was the old coin that he had found on Assateague. It was still crusted with sand in places, but the shiny parts glinted in the candlelight. Willa wanted to ask Ben if he had made a wish, but she told herself it didn't really matter.

"I hope so too," Willa agreed.

The dining room was full. The other four

tables all had guests. Everyone was talking and eating and smiling.

"Look, place cards," Ben said, pointing. "With our names."

Willa hardly even remembered making the practice cards with their names; Mom must have found them. Willa looked around. The room really did look amazing. She had been so busy, she hadn't realized just how much they had all done. But now she could see the signs of all their hard work.

Katherine brought out salads with ripe strawberries, snap peas, and corn-bread croutons. Then she came back, this time with fresh-squeezed lemonade.

"Wow, this place is nice," Ben said.

"Yeah, it is," Willa agreed. It felt cozy. It felt

welcoming. As she lifted her glass, she noticed Mom and Dad standing in the doorway to the kitchen. They had lemonade too. "Turn around," she told Ben.

Ben did, and then the Dunlaps all raised their glasses and took a sip.

The lemonade was just how Willa liked it, not too sour or too sweet.

"Here's to Misty Inn," Ben said.

"And to our home," Willa added, and they both took another sip.

KRISTIN EARHART grew up in Worthington, Ohio, where she spent countless waking and sleeping hours dreaming about horses and ponies. Eventually she took riding lessons and had her own pony . . . then her own horse. They were two of the best friends a girl could have. These days she lives in Brooklyn, New York, with her husband and son, who are also her good friends. She has a sweet and surly cat—but no horse, at least for now.

♥

Marguerite Henry's Misty Inn is inspired by the award-winning books by **Marguerite Henry**, the beloved author of such classic horse stories as *King of the Wind*; *Misty of Chincoteague*; *Justin Morgan Had a Horse*; *Stormy, Misty's Foal*; *Misty's Twilight*; and *Album of Horses*, among many other titles.